Elizabeth Mary Parsons

**Routine;**

Or, a Tale of the Goodwin Sands, etc. etc.,

Elizabeth Mary Parsons

**Routine;**
*Or, a Tale of the Goodwin Sands, etc. etc.,*

ISBN/EAN: 9783744791366

Printed in Europe, USA, Canada, Australia, Japan

Cover: Foto ©Andreas Hilbeck / pixelio.de

More available books at **www.hansebooks.com**

# ROUTINE;

OR,

# 𝔄 𝔗𝔞𝔩𝔢 𝔬𝔣 𝔱𝔥𝔢 𝔊𝔬𝔬𝔡𝔴𝔦𝔫 𝔖𝔞𝔫𝔡𝔰,

ETC. ETC.

# POEMS

BY

## ELIZABETH MARY PARSONS,

AUTHOR OF "THE END OF THE PILGRIMAGE,"
ETC. ETC.

London:

## CHARLES WESTERTON,

PUBLISHER,

27, ST. GEORGE'S PLACE, HYDE PARK CORNER.

1861.

# DEDICATION.

———◆———

Knowing my offering is little worthy the kindly notice of one so talented, whose works are so justly appreciated by the public, that one admirer more or less must be matter of indifference; but as a trifling acknowledgment of the kind sympathy and helpful encouragement so liberally accorded to one unknown to fame,

## This little Volume is Dedicated

TO THE AUTHOR OF

"WHITEFRIARS," "RICHELIEU IN LOVE," &c., &c.,

with genuine admiration and affectionate friendship,

by

THE AUTHOR.

# PREFACE.

Is a book better with or without a Preface ? And with what object is it generally written? To elucidate what is obscure, or to veil in mystery what the reader would otherwise have supposed clear: to invoke admiration where no one would have dreamt of bestowing it, or deprecate harsh judgment upon some weak point that might, but for the unlucky preface, have escaped general censure, and only been formidable in the hands of the critics; perhaps even to apologize for taking the liberty of publishing at all, which meanness of self-appreciation justly invokes the ire of all,—for who ever writes a book they do not think worth reading, and if so, what right have they to burden the public with it prefaced or unprefaced ? I have proposed to myself none of these. My little volume must go forth and win or lose, uninfluenced by any farther help or hindrance of mine; for having done my present best, I am prepared to take the consequences, hoping that my future best may be an advance towards that perfection we must all so vainly try to reach. Even praise, to be acceptable, must come from a right quarter, or it degenerates into the bitterest condemnation; and the censure or sarcasm of some is as a crown of thornless roses : enough that it has not been sought in any by the present writer, and should it be unexpectedly evoked, it will come as a pleasant surprise, the sweeter that it was unlooked for.

The first and second Poems form a striking contrast. Whether the first foreshadows the Future, portrays the Present, or really belongs to a bygone century, or how much of it in any time could come within the limits of possibility, the reading public are in a position to adjudge for themselves; but I fear me the Lord Routine starved not, but is still to be held accountable for some of our worst mishaps. The second Poem shows what the Boats of the *Royal National Life-boat Institution*\* can do when manned by our brave Sailor Volunteers; their heroism making it at once our duty as a nation, and our pleasure as individuals, to place at its disposal funds that will plant like Boats at points along our coasts wherever needed,—we all know that a Crew will be forthcoming. Let us hope their gallant efforts may be blessed with aid from above, as they have hitherto so signally been. For the remaining Poems, as for these two, " *Honi soit qui mal y pense.*"

These few observations made, the short-lived preface comes to an end. Is it untimely? and should it not hvae been begun? *N'importe!* I say thus much for it—if you have read it—don't; if you have not—do.

---

\* I have since learned that the Ramsgate Life-boat does not belong to the *Institution*; a sight of the orders issued respecting it, and a knowledge of the catastrophe that occurred in the early part of the present year, detailed in the *Daily Telegraph* and other papers, must make it a source of congratulation alike to its Members and the Public that it does not.

# CONTENTS.

# ROUTINE;

## OR,

# A TALE OF THE GOODWIN SANDS.

⊠

OW one hundred years ago ;
Ten decades of buried years.
Marching by demand our tears.

Passed they fast, or passed they slow,—
We are wand'ring on their track,
On their coffins we go back.

Strange to us the tales they tell,—
We will listen now to one,
Though we sorrow ere 'tis done ;

B

Weeping o'er what then befel,
Nine-and-ninety steps we take,
So the hundredth year we wake.

List ! a voice takes up the tale,
Will our smiles or tears prevail ?

Old the speaker, worn with care,
Sin and sorrow written there.

Blanched his cheek, bowed is his head,
Round he looks with air of dread.

Shriveled skin and sunken eye,
Seeking ours but to defy,
    As he scowling says with ire :

" I have come at your desire,—
Why disturb the buried years,
Only to call forth your tears ?

Maudlin tears ye like to shed,
Thinking ye bewail the dead.

" Weeping for yourselves I trow,
Much more to the purpose now ;
Yet since ye will have it so,
Listen to a tale of woe,
One that happened long ago."

Snarling sure had been his trade,
Ever since the world was made ;

Yet he dropt his vengeful eye,
And began full dreamily.—

" We will to the castle go,
As the ramparts we walk slow,
Ye shall learn a legend there :
Desolate the city fair,
Past all trace of it away,

" Though it once was glad and gay ;

   Sandown Castle lonely stands,

     As a warning to all lands ;

   Ye shall learn the reason why

   The curse fell so heavily.


" It was a New Year's Night, serene and calm ;

No storms abroad, the winds were hushed to rest,

Or only heard, as, breathing in her sleep

Nature sighed softly on the lap of night,

Whose sable curtains, sweeping round her bed,

Guard all the infant essences, that morn

Will sweetly kiss and startle into life.


" O life ! O death ! morning and evening chime—

Dark midnight, and bright noontide's merry glow ;—

The golden sun—and the sweet silver moon

With all attendant stars—the earth—the sea—

All old worlds and all new in ev'ry sphere—
Dissolve in chaos, ere the mystery
Of this one night comes forth to human ken :
Baffling an overburdened soul to know
How much of truth's unsought-for germ may lie
In the full kernel of a midnight dream.

"The Harbour-master slumb'ring in his chair
In most perplext unrest, says ' Untergang : '
The dying shriek of six-and-twenty men
Appal the speaker, and the scene is changed.

" His soul, released by sleep in mimic death,
Made a mere puppet of its tenement,
And leant a willing ear to such strange sounds,
To sights so wild and so incredible
Was witness, yet so true it seemed withal,
That trembling oft he solemnly averred,
He was no sleeper cozened by a dream,

But saw and felt and heard what other men,
Had they had hydra lives, could ne'er have done
And lived.

        " For him, past is the quiet night,
He hears the raging of the storm without,—
He dreams the waves demand in angry tone
The lives of a whole struggling foreign crew
Ashore upon the Goodwin ; and the fiend
In shape of dastard pride, said : ' Let them die,
The messenger from Deal was not to thee.'—
Then whispered narrow-minded, lank Routine,
Swathed in the red tape that had maimed its sires,
Crippled its own fair limbs, and shewn the world
How trammelled minds move years in the same groove :
' Instructions bear you out, you will be safe,
Wait till they shew a light from Beacon Head,
It so was named in orders from Blackhole.'
He took the two ideas and made them one,
Else he had not contained them, and he saw

His puerile self alone, in darkness sat,
Beneath the shadow of his dignity :—
In vain did Samuel Perrin's well-known voice
Plead for the crew of the doomed ' Untergang.'
There was the gallant lifeboat ready manned,
Impatient hearts were leaping at the task,
But—monstrous deed—they were denied her aid :
The Harbour-master's sullen voice said, ' *No.*'
And indignation filled the sailors' breasts
As, ordered from the boat, they homeward went ;
Blushing for very shame at the foul thought,
That one in human shape could surely know
The frantic suff'rings of a drowning crew,
And calmly wait while the encroaching storm
Bellowed its orgies in their frighted ears,
And death made ready to receive his prey.

" Pass on, brave men, ye are indeed absolved,
No voice will be uplifted save in praise

That ye were ready, and had saved their lives,
But that official ignorance stepped in,
And—the old story—rusted in the blood,
And paralysed each noble thought and deed.

" For two whole hours, (he dreamed,) he waited on,
With strange misgivings gnawing at his heart,
That he had wrongly done ; yet once denied,
Not all the prayers of the whole sailor race,
Nor all the messengers that Deal could send,
Nor sweet humanity's half-stifled voice,
Could change his purpose.
                              " 'T was bordering on nine,
When the bright signal came from Beacon Head.   .

"Those precious minutes that had winged their flight
To join Eternity, had borne with them
The means to save.   Near two o'clock they came
From off a bootless errand, all too late

For any saving purpose; yet, O God,
Inscrutable in judgment! in their ears
Oft tingled the wild death-cry of that crew:
Long were their eyes as blasted by the sight
Of that doomed vessel found'ring in the tide.
They cruised about in vain—no life was saved—
That night no human form by them was seen,
Save their own half-distracted, weary selves,
Till they returned with their sad tale of woe;
And ' Untergang ' became a name of dread.

" The Harbour-master slunk as smitten hound.—
Before the month was out the public voice
Was roused to hoot him from his place of pow'r;
And though he paced with haughty mien among
His fellows, dreaded he his Lord's return.
He knew that thousands breathed his name in scorn,
And looked with loathing each to each, and said:
' Are we on English ground? Can this be true?'

Men's tongues were utt'ring judgment loud and deep ;
Some cursed him for a hardened fiend, but some
Whispered, ' incompetent '—and many said :
' Though fearful was their fate—*The Twenty-six*—
' Yet rather would they suffer the death-throes
' Of the whole number drawn into one pang,
' Than be the man who sent them to their doom.'


   " Day after day went by, no tidings came
Of tell-tale bodies cast upon the shore ;
The orphan'd children of a widowed sire
Ne'er congregated round his shrouded corpse—
Dead or alive, in vain Deal claimed her own,
For William Johnson to a living crew
Was never Pilot, from that fearful night
When the Earl Godwin with his spectral hand
Clutched at his throat, and shook his weird white locks
To blind him, that he might not see how near
To his Estate he was ; for he had need

Of victims; madly thirsting for their lives,
Insatiate ever; the obedient sand
Made common cause with him, and drew down all,
Alike the pilot with the murdered crew.


  " Days became weeks, but still there seemed no
        change.
He lived through public obloquy that clung
Tenacious of its object; ev'ry sum
Announced for Johnson's children, seemed a goad
To prick him into shame.   But he was dull,
And clung to office with a desp'rate gripe;
If not kicked thence he would hold on till death
With his numbed fingers, and he gained the day;
His absent Lord was deaf to pleading tongues
That would have ousted him,—*his place he kept.*


  " Weeks mounted into months, (for still his dream
In life-like semblance carried him along,)

Till once again a New Year's day was born;
And then to stifle thought, he filled his house,
Nor counted o'er his guests, 'till ranged around
At well spread table, as the lightning's flash
Across the brain, he noted to himself
The fated number of THE TWENTY-SIX!


" 'T was seven o'clock, the very hour at which,
One year agone, he said that sullen ' *No.*'
And fear fell on him, doubt, dread, mystery,
A perplex feeling—that it was not chance
Had wielded such a homethrust at his heart;
But far beyond his ken, some other pow'r,
Beneath whose influence he felt chilled and strange,
Was surely there at work ;—the company
In their hilarity seemed checked, and stared
Each at some other with a hushed, awed look,
That tokened naught of good, a boding gleam
Of evil to befal them—undefined.—

(Who would not rather face the worst their fate

In its malignest vengeful ire can bring,

Than bow, with palsied heart and blenching frame,

Before the shadow of some dread unknown?)

'T was as some ghost had passed, and the chill air

Had struck their vitals, with a deadlier cold

Than bleak Siberia's most chilling frost;

In vain they tried to rally, as their host

With perturbation ordered fuel on,

Until in seeming joy, the sparkling flame

Leaped up, and cracked as Christmas yule-logs should

When merry faces form a setting bright:—

'Twas as sharp, gibing mockery to them.

In vain the smoking viands were consumed,

With good rich wines, whose luscious names have pow'r

To warm cold hearts, with stirring memories

Of jovial feasts, when they were toasted round,

For those bright eyes and laughing ruby lips,

That pouting scorned them with so haught an air.

Bacchus himself grew powerless, and paled
His ruddy cheeks, as minutes lived and died,
Bequeathing hours, each with a dying speech
From the inexorable tell-tale clock,
Whose rich sonorous voice sent harmony
From out its marble black in ghostly chime;
As some deluded nun in sable robe,
Chanting, by aid of beads, her deathlike prayer—
E'en while she counts by inches wanes the soul.

" As ev'ning sank into the shades of night,
The Harbour-master, weary of his guests,
Would fain dismiss them, but they took no hint,
And gradually one by one they slept—
Such a strange sleep—so much more near to death
In semblance, than the kindly rest we take;
No quiet respiration heaved their breasts,
Nor did the eyelid shield the weary orb,
Spell-bound—entranced—but not as living men

Waking or sleeping.

                  " A most ghastly group
Of hideous statuary, cut in hell
By some malignant sculptor, who on earth
Debased his heaven-born art to the corrupt,
And now was fiendish in his hate for men,
In fash'ning such had won his Master's praise;
But naught of nature's limning seemèd there—
Yet slowly, by degrees, they changed again.

  " With wild dilated eye, and ev'ry nerve
In fullest tension, with suspended breath,
The wretched host sat palsied in his chair,
While slowly, slowly, scarce perceptibly,
But oh, so surely, ev'ry man was changed
Into some other, and he looked around
For one familiar face, in vain, in vain ;—
E'en their habiliments had altered, for
In sailors' garb they sat—*a foreign crew.*

" One Englishman alone confronted him
With pale set face, as though the waves had washed
And eddy'ng round it had refined its mould,
And giv'n it the polished, smoothened, well-worn,
Surface of the stones, cast up in play-day,
High on the happy, prattling, sunny beach ;
But well he knew while gazing, that no play
Had sent that Spirit there, for such he was
He doubted not, though all unknown to him
While he had lived and breathed—some inward voice
Pervaded his whole being with one name—
Each fibre shook, each nerve re-echoed back,
And ev'ry vein swelled as it were with sound—
Till from his own parched lips, self-moving, came
What most he feared to hear—'WILLIAM JOHNSON.'

" ' The Murderer,' said the awful visitant,
' Manslayer of these five-and-twenty men
' Who trusted me,—who but for me had left

' In open boat, to whom the angry waves

' Would sure have been more merciful than I :

' The mate with only four now live to tell

' That they escaped ; ' Plenty of room,' they said,—

' Aye, truly there was room, but I said ' No ' :

' I would have drowned them too, I pleaded sore

' For their return.—Why ? think you, why ? '

                         " He paused ;

Each eye was turned on him with wond'ring gaze,

But no one ventured in the silence drear,

Expostulation, soothment for reply.


" ' Why ? ' he said, once again, and then the word

Swelled in it's import to a threat'ning roar ;

For well the shrinking Harbour-master felt

Impeachment, and his sentence too were there

Biding an answer ; and he met the eye

Of the Deal pilot with the cow'ring dread

That dastard souls at sight of Justice feel.

                           c

"' Come Heav'n to witness though I did the deed,'
Johnson then said, and raised his hand on high :
' It was to save them ;—wherefore risk our lives
' Upon that raging surf in open boat,
' When safety would be brought us well I knew,
' By the brave Sandown far-famed Boat and Crew.
' This was my fault, I paid it with my life ;
' But list, they manned the Boat,—do you deny
' They manned her ?'
                        "And he gasped out, ' No.'
' You say the word that slew us ; when the men
' Impetuous flew to aid, (O gallant hearts,
' I well might trust them,)—when they filled the Boat
' And would have saved us, Master, you said, ' No,'
' That word our death : we waited on and on,
' At first in confidence, as high and bold,
' As if already, on the raging sea,
' We had beheld the white-winged Harbinger,
' Of safety well assured ; as time wore on

' We drooped to hope,—our misery was great,

' To agony it grew,—the hours went by,

' Till suff'ring lashed us into wild despair,

' And then the final End, when all went down ;

' Our last breath sharper drawn, with keener woe,

' That none had tried to save us—e'en ourselves

' Had thrown away a latent chance of life—

' In this, where rests the blame ?   Is it on me

' Because I trusted English hearts and hands,

' And with my own life testified my faith ?

' Or is't on thee, who cruel to the last,

' Denied all help, yet art alive and free ?


" ' For one whole year upon my soul has lain

' The fearful cry of these poor murdered men ;

' I come to right myself, to let them know

' That I had warrant for my confidence

' In these my fellows, who had manned the boat,—

' To let them know that Johnson never lied

' To them, but was himself, in evil hour,

' Betray'd by thee—the most accurst of men;

' Who for no motive, but a stiff-necked pride

' Of office, *for the which thou wert not fit,*

' Sent me, thy fellow-countryman, and these—

' Who being strangers were more sacred still—

' To such a death as e'en brave men may fear.


" ' This is the man, drowned Germans, but for whom

' Ye had been safe as any on the sea.'


" The Harbour-master shrank as ev'ry eye

Of that weird, spectral crew turned full on him.

It was a ghastly sight; yet close his eyes

He could not, while that fearful stony glare

Was on him.

               " ' You will know him once again ?'

The Pilot said ; the sailors muttered ' Ja '

In strong assent, and to each other turned,

Their foreign clamor wild'ring all around
As, with hoarse voice, they judged him and condemn'd.


" ' Hast aught to say in thy defence, O man ? '
Said the stern spokesman of the twenty-six.


" So called upon, he moved, and trembling said :
' I sent the Boat, although it came too late.
' No fault of mine was that.   They showed no Light
' From off the Beacon Head, to ask for aid,
' Till' nearly nine, and then I sent the Boat.
' From Deal to Samuel Perrin message came
' Full two hours earlier, true ;—but what of that?
' *'Twas not official—therefore not for me.*
' And that I did no wrong all men may see ;—
' I acted upon orders, and am here
' As Harbour-master still.—No murderer I.'


" His self-accusing speech the German crew

Received with mocking laugh, with gibe, and jest.

Amongst themselves, with fearful scorn, they said,

That to foul murder he joined suicide :

And then sat silent, with attentive mien,

To watch their leader ;—soon he spoke again :


" ' You sent the Boat in time for them to hear

' The Death-shriek, of the *six-and-twenty men*

' They pleaded hard to save.   Their own dear lives,

' As nothing in the balance held, they risked

' For us ;  and as for hours they cruised about,

' Passed and repassed our pallid corpses o'er,

' As they lay strewn at bottom of the sea.

' Not one e'er visited the English shore,

' To be in churchyard laid with Christian prayer.

' Our graveyard, sacred to ourselves alone,

' With ocean-flowers to deck it—not cold stones

' That scare the passer-by, like convict gangs,

' Sending a shudder through the stoutest heart :

‘ And for our *In Memoriam*,—ev'ry weed,

‘ With ev'ry shell cast idly on the beach,

‘ Tells our sad tale, and touches to the core

‘ The many who have loved us.　Years to come,

‘ When my poor children send their little ones

‘ To play upon the coast, mayhap they'll say :

‘ ‘ Go, seek what Grand-dad sends you from the sea ! ’

‘ And if the tears wrung from me at the thought

‘ Of what their orphaned childhood must endure,

‘ Like oysters, turn to pearls, the tiny hands

‘ Will oft take home a treasure from their sire.


“ ‘ Poor miserable driv'ller !　who could doom

‘ With solemn pomp of power ;　and stop to con

‘ What was the strictest letter of the law

‘ While human life was in the balance held.

‘ Has no one judged thee ?—not the public voice

‘ Of brave old England ?　Was the *Press* struck dumb,

‘ And uttered forth no protest in the ears

‘ Of the whole Nation, when so foul a wrong

‘ Was told throughout the land ?   I tell you—yes !

‘ And has been heard on high, mingling with ours ;

‘ And as annihilation cannot be to aught,

‘ It dies not, but is echo'ng through all space;

‘ Nor will stay its cry till thou inhale it

‘ With a breath, that sobbing, asks forgiveness

‘ From thine offended Country and thy God !


“ ‘ Never again will mine accusing voice

‘ Sound in thine ears, till at the crack of doom;

‘ Then, if Repentance have not stirred thy soul,

‘ Shudder to think this visit was in vain.

‘ In judgment, mercy is remembered still;—

‘ Yet on each New Year's Night there is for thee

‘ A fearful penance, that will never cease—

‘ Will never fail to claim thee, till the hour

‘ When, with just loathing for thy heinous sin

‘ 'Gainst all humanity that cleaves to thee,

‘ Thou shalt be Harbour-master here no more.

‘ Yet not in malice is the sentence passed—

‘ As a reminding call to thee,—‘ Repent,’

‘ That I but bring to thee as instrument

‘ Of One who errs not when he deals with men.


“ ‘ Each New Year's Night, on board a Phantom-ship,

‘ By name the ‘ Untergang,’ thou wilt be wrecked ;

‘ Thy fate most dismal—thou wilt die alone,

‘ And at the bottom of the sea wilt find

‘ Our tell-tale bodies ;—thou to each wilt say :

‘ ‘ God give thee peace, my brother ! ’ and pass on

‘ To live amongst thy fellows ; yet return

‘ To do the like again—else we sleep not :

‘ Each year, till ye repent, and office yield

‘ To one more worthy, this shall be thy doom !’


“ Noiseless as they had entered, these strange men,

So did they now depart ;—the rigid look,

The stony, ghastly stare, returned again,
With all attendant horrors of the scene ;
For as each one passed from their lifeless Life
To deathless Death, by calm and passionless
Transition, they took up the Pilot's words
In parrot-like rotation ;—for to them
They had no meaning, save that to their ear
There had been menace in the tone of him
Who spake ;  so each one said, with threat'ning look
And foreign accent, ' This shall be thy doom ! '
Then sat immovable, in seeming dead :
The Pilot's calm AMEN confirm'd the words
In all their fearful import, and he groaned
Aloud, the only living man the room
Contained,—for so it seemed awhile to him :
Yet when he looked again, he knew them all ;
His own friends compassed him about, and laughed
That he had slept so long.

                 " But he smiled not,

For he was puzzled in his sleep to know
How this could be; nor did it seem to him
That he had dreamed;—he felt he must have lived
And acted out the drama on this earth—
The keen reality was still so fresh.
Yet when they swore that they had never changed,
But only he had slept, he 'gan to doubt,
And dreamed that he had dreamed.

                " Tis passing strange,
These errant moods in sleep, when our poor selves
Become the objects of our vain regard,
And we can speculate in mystic thought
E'en in our dreams, if we have dreamed or no.


" They told him he had slept, and his crazed brain
Accepted it for truth, feeling relief,
Yet ever and anon misdoubted it;
And shudd'ring said, 'Next New Year's Night will
    prove.'

" So he woke not—but in his vision lived—
Thought—spoke—and acted out a year—that seemed
To him the ordinary length of months
A year should be.

               " For in our dreamy sleep,
We weave from out the woof of Father Time
Or much or little, as it seemeth good
To us—of minutes we make months or years—
Or we compress these last to atomies—
Living long lives, and fashioning events,
That waking, we have never dared to hope
Would rise upon our path to make us blest ;
Or conjuring such wild, despairing sights,
As even the dread mystery of Life
(We thank our Heavenly Father) fails to bring ;
Yet open our 'mazed eyes to find that we,
So often duped, misled, betrayed, hoodwinked
By others, must ourselves befool with dreams :
One little hour we scarce have slept away—

Yet oh ! to think that the whole tide of life
May never bring to fever-parching lips
So sweet a draught of nectar as the gods
That wait on Sleep in dreams oft hand to us ;
One that the roughnesses of daily toil
Can never dash away—*it once was ours ;*
What matters it that we deceived ourselves,
If it brought happiness that real seems
As aught our waking hours can give to us,
When we are building equally on sand
Trusting our fellows ?
       " So we marvel out
That to our God a thousand years should seem
As one short day, or that the smaller space
Of four-and-twenty hours to thousand years
Should lengthen out, when his own gift of Sleep
Lays gentle hand on us, and almost works
A miracle as great.
       " And New Year's Day

Received its breath of life,—another wave
From the unfathomable, shoreless sea
Of God's Eternity broke on the shore
Of this our little world, and kissed our feet,
As if with hope to strengthen for the toil
It knew lay hid behind.

                " But the bright light
Of this same New Year's Day with agony
The Dreamer shunned,—declared it was not morn,
And closed his eyes—in vain—his mind had seized
Upon the fact—the lids but shut it in,
And banishing externals, gave full scope
To its vague terrors, working for itself
Such problems for the ending of the day,
That he e'en blessed the light he cursed before,
And prayed it not to leave him.

                  " But the world
Revolved, as was its wont, and darkness fell
On land and sea, but on his spirit most;

As the light waned, he sickened in his fear
To abject cowardice, prayed to bare walls
To witness, he would office hold no more,
That he resigned—had meant to do long since—
Would Harbour-master never be again
While he drew breath ; his terror came too late
For saving pow'r ; each minute only brought
His punishment the nearer, and his wild,
Excited efforts to escape but made
His frame the feebler, to endure the doom
That glided toward him, till he felt its fang,
As the envenomed serpent's deadly gripe,
Deep—deep—and then the poison's mad wild gush
Through all his veins.   He started up,
And gasping forth, ' My doom, my doom,' rushed out
As though he fled from demons.

                              . " To the pier
He went, when, as he neared the end athwart
His path, stood Samuel Perrin,—in the flesh

Was he, stalwart as ever, yet he said
Words of strange import.

       " ' If you're wrecked to-nigl
' No Life-boat leaves the port, you're best at home ;
' On New Year's Night, while you are master here,
' There's not a soul dares man her, mark you this–
' We've all been cautioned of the Phantom-ship
' That haunts the Goodwin, and not one will stir
' To save you ; 'twas e'en on such a night as this
' The ' Untergang ' went down: yet *there she rides*
' As waiting for a Pilot.'

       " Then he saw
'Twas even as the other said, the ship
Awaited him ; and he shrieked forth, ' My doom !'
And onward went to meet it.

       " ' Pilot I
' On board the ' Untergang ?'   No, never ; Death
' Were welcome rather.   I defy my doom,
' And all the fiends that forged it.'

" With these words
Into the raging sea he sprang ; the waves,
With forked white tongues, licked round the pier, and
    threw
Their giant arms wide open to receive
And buffet him ; 't would comfort be to toss
Amid their grim caressing—so he thought ;
But even as he fell, a little boat
Shot forward, seemingly propelled by chance,
And so received him that he had no hurt,
And seemed to have no fall ; it was as if
He had stept in from off the Harbour stairs
In quiet mood.   He cursed the boat, and swore
Many a fearful oath, which helped him not.
But wicked rage, when impotent to harm,
Will vent itself in curses : on he went,
Or curse, or bless, it had been all the same,
For no one heard him ; he made not the air
Pestiferous for others e'en to breathe
With his foul language, only for himself

D

Was it so loaded; and the shrieking wind
Made fitting symphony as it gushed by
On deeds of vengeance.

              " Still the little boat
Lived out the waves, and steadily went on,
As though in mid-day and the deadest calm
That ever settled on the changeful sea;
Rode high upon their crests, and then dived down
To nestle in their hollows, rose again,
And ever and anon he heard the oars
In mellow time-kept stroke; yet saw he not
The hands that held them.

              " Soon they neared the Ship,
And he no longer wrestled with his fate,
But clomb her side obedient as a child,
To act as Pilot for the unseen crew;
His ev'ry word responded to with ease
By them, who, silent-working, noiseless stept,
Till his whole soul was so appalled and stung
To such a sense of weariness and awe,

Combined with, heav'n only knows how much
Of supernat'ral mystery and fear,
That though he knew the danger lurking there
Boding destruction, if he bated aught
Of his keen watchfulness, he closed his eyes;
And the next moment on the Goodwin Sands
Lay the doomed ' Untergang' a cloven wreck,
While round him passed a long, low, mocking laugh,
And six-and-twenty forms flashed out as light,
Each in a Lifeboat floating from the Ship.

" 'Twas then no feint the warning he had had,
And he must die alone—a hideous death !—

" Not the slow wane of worn-out tissues,
That to the blood no longer could supply
The needful aliment; not the decay
Of nature's forces drooping to a grave ;
Nor the more cunningly devised approach
Of the Pale Monarch, when he strikes us down,

Giving no time to urge a single plea
To lengthen out existence; a fierce voice
Yells out the summons, we but hear and go !

"Would God that any one of these had been
His fate in mercy sent; he waited hours
For certain death, in a full flush of life,
.And ardent wish to live—with ev'ry pulse
In vig'rous prime of manhood—as he tried
To summon him assistance from that shore
On which he stood, when he denied the aid
Of Lifeboat to the shipwrecked crew.

                                  " They sued
In vain for help; their Beacon-lights were seen
As his from far, wild streaming to the sky;
As vainly his burned on,—the lurid flare
But added horror to the frightful scene,
And showed the waves as they grew fierce and strong,
Surging and moaning, roaring, clamoring,
Like a mad mob for a detested life.

Then terror-stricken, penitent too late,
He realized the doom to which he sent
His fellows, but one short year ago.

                  " Ah !
What would he then have given to recall
Those dead men back to life ?   To place them there—
There—where he suffered ; not that they might die,
But time be given him in which to save :
*It was too late.*

             " His heart was not the first
That has succumbed ; his life was not alone
In paying forfeit at the stern command
Of words so pitiless as these—Too LATE !
Did ever language coin them with the thought
That human hearts could hear them and live on ?


  " Too late to make repair ; too late to beg
Forgiveness from dead lips ; too late to see
Undone the evil we made haste to do :
Then break sad heart, it is too late to live ;

Snap, cords of life, as does the tuneful harp,

When cold ungenial air upon its strings

Makes mournful inroads, and in breaking—die ;

If so, sweet harmony may be restored :

Better a thousand times to yield the soul,

Than make discordant sounds with a marred life,

That will but tangle and knot up the threads

Of kindred lives, that otherwise were free.


"And all too late would our lost dreamer here

The German crew to life recall ; in vain

Would he his own soul give for those who sleep

Beneath ; e'en as he thought upon their fate,

His own commingled.

                     "With despairing shriek

He was submerged, yet struggled fierce and strong :

His efforts fainter grew—the pang passed by ;

And with returning life he saw around,

In peaceful sleep, the Pilot and the Crew,

That in the ' Untergang,' at his command,

A wat'ry grave had found; he passed each by
With heartfelt sorrow as he wept the words,
' God give thee peace, my brother.'
  " All around
Were shells and tangle, flow'rs in tender wreaths
Twined o'er their hands and heads with loving fold,
And they looked blissful in their Ocean tomb,
Biding a judgment that he dared not face.


" He walked full carefully when—O horror!—
Stumbling he fell, and yawning to receive,
The quicksand earth with jaws wide open stood,
He fell—down—down.
  " The pit was fathomless;
He passed through all the layers of the Earth's
Encrusted surfaces, and then he felt
From one vast chaos rush the liquid fire;
The glowing element at furnace heat
Roared towards him; madness came on, suggesting
How, in volcanic stream, his calcined bones

Should with fierce lava blend, and be cast forth
From out the centre of the earth, to bring
Death and destruction on his fellow-men,
Rejected e'en by her who brought him forth.


" The white heat sprang with fierce velocity,
And wrapped him round in one vast coil of flame ;
He shrieked, and moving as he writhed in fire,
Struck on the chair, and striking, he awoke.


" Low—low—had burned the fire,
    As it had been a fun'ral pyre ;
    Sob—sob—the moaning wind,
    As it had left the dead behind ;
    Weep—weep—the falling rain,
    As hoping to efface the stain.


" Die fire—pale ashes fall,
    Fittest emblem for a pall ;

Sob wind—most surely you
Stricken mourner for the crew ;
Weep rain—with secret dread,
Tearful o'er Despair's soft tread.

" Neither fire—wind—nor rain,
Ever could assuage his pain ;
He might never live to be
From that fearful vision free.

" Strange the Vision—as it sped,
Each one looked in fear and dread ;
Stranger still what then befel,
Scarce believe you what I tell;
As I speak your sceptic face
Hardens, leaves of faith no trace ;
But more marvellous than all
Was the judgment then to fall."

Pausing here, the Ancient Man
Communed with himself a span,

Older looked and more bowed down,
With an ever-deep'ning frown,
Yet it seemed as born of thought,
Not by vengeful passion wrought.


Inward pond'ring o'er his theme,
Suddenly there shot a gleam ;
'Cross his dark'ning visage passed
Fire of youth that could not last,
Bright'ning up and flaming there,
As the Night Wind stirred his hair.


And forget I never can
Figure of that Ancient Man.


When he once more spoke again,
One hand he stretched o'er the main,
One hand he waved toward the plain ;
Lifeless they fell down again.

Still less will his story fade,
From the strong impression made :
While the billows round us played,
He his tale once more essayed.

" Think you that the Master *dreamed?*
Hath not Truth for ever seemed
Far more troublous, weird, and wild,
Than strange Fiction's flighty child?
How much was truth I will not say,
But somewhat on his conscience lay.

" Look toward the Goodwin—weep to know
The six-and-twenty sleep below ;
Look toward the plain—and sigh to think
That we are standing on the brink
Of a dead City's nameless grave,
Where lived the coward and the brave.

" The Harbour-master erred because
He blindly followed out the laws ;

For by the *letter* he was led,
The *spirit* of the text lay dead;
Not brains enough had he to see
That, in such dire extremity,
The knowledge that he had obtained
Was quite as good as if he'd gained
From Beacon Head the fearful news,
Of stranded ships and sinking crews.

" But some men surely are born fools,
And can but work as senseless tools.
The blame attaches then to those,
Who place them where each wind that blows
May turn them wrong as soon as right,
The misery on others light;
But least of all their plaything be
Of Human Life upon the sea.

" The Lord Routine was dastard worse,
And on him heaviest fell the curse;

For though he knew the Master failed,
He felt he was himself assailed;
He must uphold his puppet,—or,
Where would be Dignity and Law?
And no drowned seamen rose to claim
From English Jury, in the name
Of their lost ship and submerged crew,
The justice to their mem'ry due;
The thing was hushed, as babe to sleep,
But in some hearts it rankled deep.

" While he with red tape bound their brains,
He might as well have spared his pains,
For as he ambled o'er his task,
From off men's minds there fell the mask;
And seeing as they ne'er had seen,
They recognised the Lord Routine:
Reproached him with his creeping pace,
That let men perish in the face
Of their brave comrades; and with means at hand,
Had thrown so deep a stigma on the land.

" The Harbour-master was removed, and then
　　In quiet slept the six-and-twenty men ;
　　The phantom ' Untergang ' was seen no more
　　For Pilot waiting, as she neared the shore :
　　　　　Although some say,
　　　　　On New Year's Day,
　　　　That you may hear the wail
　　　　　Of German fraus,
　　　　　On lifeboat prows,
　　　　And see a German sail.


" The Lord Routine, they starved to death
　　Within his castle here ;
　　Not one looked pity'ng on his fate,
　　Not one ere shed a tear.


" The City seemed as a disgrace,
　　A monument of shame ;
　　And so they razed it to the ground,—
　　Buried the ghost of blame.

" And Heav'n with favor viewed the deed :
 For when the winter snow
Fell lightly, and dissolved again,
 Gone was the scene of woe.

" As a magician's wand had been
 The winding-sheet of snow,
For not a stone was left behind
 Save on the beach below ;
The Harbour silted up with sand
And merged into a pebbly strand.

" The Castle as a curse was left,
 And Lord Routine of life bereft
  Found there a lonely tomb ;
But once a year returns to life,
And hears the shriek of wailing wife
  Above the waters' boom.

" Only once has he been seen,
 Only once been heard ;

You alone with his corpse have been,
Or have his spirit stirred.


" Ev'ry century a ghost
Leaves for landmark on the coast ;
I am one and I bide here,
Castle Sandown is my bier.


" Lifeless I, but for your call,
I have answered once for all :
None on earth o'er me have pow'r
Dead am I as strikes the hour.


" Lord Routine's expiring voice,
Dies with me beyond all choice ;
I for ever silent cower,
Lonely as Martello Tower.


" Oft to Castle Sandown come,
Often ponder o'er the ' Doom.'

Come ye often to my bier
None will ever find me here;
Spirit only none can see,
And such only I shall be."


Slowly vanished into air,
I alone was standing there;
But forget I never can
Figure of that Ancient Man.


Silence fell on all around
As I paced the haunted ground,—
Weird and spectral all things seemed;
Round about the Castle gleamed
Lights as from a city fair,
Yet nor house nor light was there;—
Busy hum of human kind
Was borne in upon the wind,
But no voice of man came near,
Desolation's self was here;

E

And the ever murm'ring sea
Chaunted sad and low to me;
In its mournful accent said,
' Moan as I do for the dead.'


Ring ! ring a doleful knell,
Let us hear the Passing Bell,
   For a Hundred years have flown.
Sing ! sing a merry song
No one dreams that we do wrong,
   For the world has wiser grown.


Sleep ! sleep in trustful peace
We have taken a new lease,
   And our lives are free and glad;
None haunt the Goodwin now,
No wrecked vessel's phantom prow,
   Looming, drives our sailors mad.

Laugh ! laugh e'en at the grave,
Surely none would try to save
   Such a wretch as Lord Routine :
Shout ! shout to think that we
Are from his dominion free ;
    'Tis a thing that once has been.

Ne'er again will England hold,
Or for silver or for gold,
   Red tape trappings high ;
Generations passed away
May have thought that they looked gay,
    Flaunting in the sky.

But our men of heart and hope
Care no more than for the Pope
   For their swathing bands ;
Past alike and torn aside
From our pathway, though we died,
    By English hearts and hands.

# THE WRECK OF THE "SAMARITANO."

 SABBATH-DAY should tell of quiet rest,
And chiming bells make winter months seem
blest;
Yet dark'ning at the fall, and moaning loud,
The pregnant wind rouses the threat'ning cloud:
The snow-squalls, white as infant's winding-sheet,
Blinding as sand, as Arab horse more fleet,
Are borne along to deck the sable night,
While shutting out dark scenes from human sight.
Moan winds—weep women—down upon your knees,
When morning dawns blood shall as water freeze;
Send up your prayers to Heav'n—God only knows
How much He will abate of human woes;

Use ye the means, and leave the rest to Him :
Such nights as these make hearts and eyes grow dim.


Go forth " Eclipse," and seek, 'midst sand and shoal,
The vessel fated ne'er to reach the goal ;
She is a Spanish brig from Antwerp bound,
But will Santander never reach,—she found
A treach'rous death-bed on the Margate Sands :
They swallow up the cargo other lands
Once deemed their own ; and threaten e'en her crew,
Who, with Capt. Modeste Crispo, look to you.
At half-past five, 'mid wild and madd'ning din,
Boats were put off—oars broken—boats stove in.
While running for the Brig they speak a Smack,
Take two men and her boat,—the tide runs slack,
And ebbs with sullen groan ; they board her then,'
And hoping when the flood shall make again
To ease her off, they leave six Margate men ;
Add the two Whitstable—in all nineteen.
But with the rising tide the sleeping gale

Renewed its fury, and with long, low wail,
Sent up the angry waves to seize their prey,
And wreck at once the vessel as she lay ;
They take her in their large dark arms with force,
They dash her on the Sands with murm'rings hoarse,
They break across the deck—they crush the boat—
Force up the hatches—and the cargo float—
The rigging's cut—the mainmast crashes down—
Still the winds whistle—still the waters frown ;
In mock'ry decking them with wreaths of snow,
Garlands of spray, and foaming columns flow ;
While drowning men by slipp'ry shroud hold on,
And shaking foremast topples to its doom :
Hour after hour with frozen hands they cling,
While round them roars the angry storm's wild din.
A wreck—a wreck.   Hail ! to the rescue, hail !
And Margate teems with life despite the gale,
That slackens not, and wearies not, but sends
The great White Horses up, and stooping bends,
And reins them in till they take forms of Death,

While lookers-on from shore hold in their breath.
The smaller Life-boat first goes out in vain,
She cannot battle with the angry main ;
Excitement had o'er-mastered watchful care,
She filled with water where there should be air ;
Her gallant crew at first took little heed,
Not prone to snatch alarm for their own need ;
A four hours' battle, and in Westgate Bay,
The Boat ashore, the men exhausted, lay.
More strength must be put forth ;—soon as they saw
One boat disabled coming back to shore ;
They man another, drag her round the Pier,
And launch her forth without one pang of fear.


" Ho ! ho !" laugh forth the giant waves at play,
" ' Friend of all Nations ' be our sport to-day ;
" We'll teach thee that we're rather rougher now
" Than when we toyed and kissed yon vessel's prow
" In times gone by ; see—we have changed our tack—
" We break thy tiller—to the shore go back."

Both wrecked.  It might be sport to the wild sea,
But it wrung human hearts with agony.
Hope, which had once beat high in ev'ry breast,
Changed into moaning, cried itself to rest;
In vain two luggers, two of goodly name,
Put forth to save, their fate was still the same ;
The " Nelson " soon came back in a sad plight,
The " Lively " too was worsted in the fight :
They could no more—Margate had done her best,
Her gallant seamen well had stood the test;
Let the stout hearts at Ramsgate only learn
How sore the need, and they will take their turn.

At Ramsgate, from an early hour, the pier
Was grouped with boatmen, knowing danger near ;
A visitor or two strays forth to see
How wild—how grand—the elements can be;
With eager glance and keen they strain their eyes,
Between the snow-squalls sadd'ning visions rise ;
In the far distance vessels run for life,

Before a gale with fell disasters rife;
The booming wind deceives the landsman's ears,
Who, shudd'ring, thinks the signal gun he hears;
The hardy sailor shakes his knowing head,
The Light-vessel for guide, he's not misled.


At nine the tidings came, a Brig on shore
Upon the Woolpack Sands off Margate,—more
They know not, but with wild excitement wait
To learn the issue; some in grave debate
About the Margate Life-boats,—they will go,
But 'gainst such fearful odds, wind, wave, and snow.


Twelve of the clock; the men to dinner go,
A few are left on watch, time passes slow;
But there is one who hies with utmost speed,
Bringing intelligence of sorest need,—
A coast-guardsman from Margate hurries by,
He tells in haste how most disastrously
Their efforts have been crowned; he craves from them

Swift help; the boatmen lose their wonted phlegm.

Scarce from the Harbour-master's lips the words

To man the Life-boat pass, but these wild birds

Are on the wing; and if the race had been

Their lives to save, not risk, you had not seen

A hotter contest; honor be to those

Who lost the race, yet gave the winners clothes,

Which in their hasty flight they failed to take,

But which their coming hardships needful make;

Cork jackets soon are thrown into the Boat,

Put on by those who are well used to float:

The pow'rful steam tug, " Aid," that night and day

In Ramsgate harbour puffs her life away;

Snorted with all her might, and her full pow'r

Put forth, as conscious of that stormy hour;

With gallant DANIEL READING in command,

Took Boat in tow and bid adieu to land;

JAMES HOGBEN, chief among that hardy crew

Of Life-boat Volunteers, his duties knew.

Now winds, as fiends shrieking, do your worst,
Black clouds that fall in white, come up and burst,
Gigantic waves fling up your angry crests,
Drench these devoted men, they've bared their breasts
To the wild fury of the vengeful three,
And they defy thy dark-browed Trinity;
Yes, come and see the victory God gives,
When men go forth to save dear human lives,—
When self-forgetting glorious Love shines out,
And clears our mental mists of sin and doubt;
For a short time by its bright light we see,
In Angel's garb, our maimed humanity.

The men bend forward with a firm strong hold,
The mittens frozen to their hands with cold;
The Steamer makes headway against the storm,
Clear of the pier they gallantly pass on.
Cud Channel, Black and White Buoys too are passed,
When heading towards them, riding on the blast,

Comes a most fearful sea ; it met and broke,
The Steamer buried in the great foam-stroke ;
The Life-boat rose and then, plunging stem on,
One moment buried, sure the men were gone,—
But no, they still are there,—a fearful strain,
And the brave Boat is sent a waif upon the main ;
The tow-rope broken, she is left to be
On broadside swamped, at mercy of the sea.

"Oars out !"—They labor, labor but in vain,
The Boat's head to the wind they cannot gain,
The gale more forceful is than they ; for fast
To the Brake Shoal they drift, as if at last
The heavy-beating sea, the snow and wind,
Burying them, would leave no trace behind.
The Boat athwart the sea in peril lies,
The Steamer to the rescue swiftly hies ;
A yard or two to windward, and they throw
Hawling-line and hawser, she's soon in tow :
The tide still flowing, rises as in wrath,

Making a deeper, blacker, deadlier path ;
The threat'ning wind comes fiercer and more fierce,
While blinding snow and sleet, that almost pierce
Marrow and vitals, freezing as they fall
Upon these sturdy heroes, make large call
For faith and courage ; see—we must look twice,
And then be doubtful—are they men or ice ?
They could not look to windward ; drifting snow,
High running seas, shut out the scene below ;
But yet not one regrets he gained the race,
And in the *Ramsgate Life:boat* took his place.


   Off Broadstairs suddenly the Boat stops way,
" Again the rope is broken," in dismay
Is the first thought ; but worse than this they see,
In its full force, their sad calamity :
The steam-tug " Aid " stops, she is broken down,
And they despair to save.
                 Does Heaven frown ?
Does God doom all those men aboard the wreck,

Spite their brave efforts, Ocean's bed to deck,
And strew with their dead bodies,—sink or swim
As the wild waters list, and at their whim?

But while they question, hope is born anew,
More cable is let out,—this is the clue
By which they know 'twas fear of such a break
Made them precautionary measures take :
Brave READING knew an enemy was nigh,
And so prepared for battle manfully ;
Struggling an hour before they reached the field,
Determined not to budge an inch or yield,
They gain the Foreland North, and there the gale
Spread with wild random fury, snow, spray, hail.

Early, and yet the light is darkened down
On such an afternoon to a dull frown ;
The captain of the Boat looks forth in vain,
He sees around naught but the angry main :
And from the " Aid" they look with straining glance,

Fearing the Boat has met with some mischance,
But nothing can they see ; she may be there
Freighted with human life, a thing of care ;
She may be there, and ev'ry man asleep
In Ocean's bed, many a fathom deep :
One hundred yards apart yet cannot tell,
If Fortune with the other dealeth well.
Passing the Foreland North the snow-squall clears,
Full many a triumph of the storm appears ;
A Lugger, foremast gone, two Life-boats wrecked,
With such sad trophies is the scene bedecked ;
And then they learn, prize to the full extent,
'Gainst what fierce odds the Margate men had bent.

Where is the Wreck ?   Are they indeed too late ?
Have the poor drowning wretches met their fate ?
To windward rolls a mass of cloud and snow,
But not a sign to tell them where to go ;
In doubt and indecision now they stand,
At last decide upon the Woolpack Sand ;

Yet scarce have done so, ere a sudden break
Shows them the Wreck for which they wish to make:
But for this help from Heav'n, ev'ry soul
Had wrung from Mother Church a passing toll.


Oh! but for God's good help, how many more
Of Ocean's sons in death would strew the shore.


The Ensign, Union downwards hath a voice,
But how to reach her?   They have little choice.
Round or across the Sand—which shall it be?
Short wavering in such extremity:
They take across the Sand, the dang'rous path,
They face the elements in all their wrath;
With a tremendous jerk the tow-rope parts,
Rejoicing they set sail.   On, gallant hearts!


Harder the gale, and the wild rush of sea,
Mad with their own pow'r, drunk with their own fury,

Join with the blinding snow, and on they drive.
The storm was at its height.　Can the Boat live?


And who shall tell the grandeur of that scene,
Who can imagine it that ne'er has been
A helpless child nursed in old Neptune's arms,
And seasoned well to all his dire alarms?


See, when he's kind, the little craft at play
Upon his heaving heart,—he seems to say :
" Sport children—gambol here and work your will,
" From my exhaustless patience take your fill;
" Upon my broad expanse you shall not see
" One harmful frown, naught but tranquillity."
But his mood changes.　Hark! what says he now,
What fate's in store for gallant barks that plough
Upon the troubled waters?　Loud he pours
Wild threat'ning words forth from his angry jaws,
His murm'rings hoarse to a fierce menace turn ;
No longer mutt'ring, his children learn

F

From the broad chest of many a beating wave
How frail is human life—how hard to save.
The Monarch Ocean in his stormy wrath
Said : " Dare ye float your cargoes on my path,
" And venture forth your precious freights of life ?
" I anger at your folly, I am rife
" For mischief, ev'ry throb of my great heart
" Shall shake your fibres—soul from body part."

The whistling wind in triumph shrieking flew,
Caught up the spray, made mocking wreaths, and threw
Columns of foam it raised, then tore them down ;
While the waves heaved and dashed with angry frown.

A cry—" Look out, my men ! hold on, hold on ! "
One moment later and the men had gone ;
Breast downward on the thwart, arms clasped around,
They wrestle with the waves that o'er them bound ;
The gallant Boat half-buried in the sea,
Like sea-gull rises in her buoyancy ;

Not once or twice, but many a time and oft
This scene repeated is, when from aloft
It seems the giant breakers heading come,
To draw down men and boat to the same doom.

Clear of the Sands more freely they take breath,
As those who have passed close to sudden death ;
Once in deep water, the huge, rolling wave,
By such comparison e'en comfort gave ;
Before the wind they put the gallant Boat,
And for the Wreck each man on the look-out.

Again by Heav'n's favor the storm breaks,
She's half-a-mile to leeward, and it makes
Their stout hearts shudder, their bronzed faces pale,
While the wind sighs a long, low, answ'ring wail ;
*So sad a sight it is*—stern on the Sands
She'd settled down, while Neptune's busy hands
Made over her a breach ; the starboard bow
Alone is visible, from stern to prow :

Foresail, foretopsail, mainmast, all were gone—
There's little left for the wild, reckless storm
To reek its fury on.
               Oh—is it so ?
Lives—there are lives who feel the keen winds blow,
Whose ev'ry breath is pain, see—one, two, three,
The rigging's full, think on their agony ;
How slow the hours have passed to tortured men,
Who never think to reach the shore again ;
Whose freezing bodies desperately cling,
Each wave to them an Emblem of Death's sting :
That tangled rigging with its freight of woe,
Obscurely seen through a thick veil of snow,
Is calculated well to touch the heart,
And from it drain its inmost selfish part.

They pass a Margate lugger lying near,
" Eight of our men on board,"—sad words to hear.

Four hours the Boat has battled with the sea ;
Eight hours have the men stayed in jeopardy.

At last the moment has arrived,—no word
Beyond a whispered order can be heard,
Risk and suspense are terr'ble ; out they pay
The cable, yard by yard, no word they say;
The waves break over them, submerge the Boat,
Rush towards the vessel, o'er the Wreck they gloat;
They hoist the sail helping the Boat to sheer,
A huge wave lifts them, they are very near,
A yard or two more cable by the run,
She is alongside and the race is won.
Three men jump in, and then a rolling wave
Threat'ning, they quickly haul the rope they gave:
They watch their chance, alongside once again,
More lives are snatched from off the hungry main.

Are they all saved ?   No, three are hanging there,
In such a state as well-nigh prompts despair ;
Their frozen limbs they scarcely can unlash
They suffer so, those cruel waves that dash
And mouth about the Boat,—the peril's great,

A few more minutes it will be too late ;
They must go close, the men too weak to leap
Are lifted as we take up those who sleep ;
And all are saved but one poor cabin boy
Entangled in the shrouds,—it is his toy,
A little bag of trinkets meant for home,
Has caught the rigging, and he cannot come ;
His small cold fingers powerless to free,
A strong hand grasps him, ere Eternity
Lays claim on all.

        See, a tremendous wave :
" Hold anchor, cable hold ! if it but gave
" One yard," there would have risen up to Heav'n
The parting cry of souls from bodies riv'n.
But no, it passes, and upon her keel
She settles down, each man as true as steel ;
Thirty-and-two now form her precious freight,
One moment for the captain's word they wait ;
" She draws away, pay out the cable, quick,
" The hatchet forward pass, quick, my men, quick."

One moment's short delay, they gash the rope,
One strand is severed, but they cannot cope
With such a fearful gust of wind as this,
Which now is borne along the wild abyss;
A crash is heard—behold the mast and sail
Are blown from out the Boat by the fierce gale.
Moment of peril !
        Towards the Wreck they drive,
On they go swiftly, helplessly they strive;
Let them but hit the Wreck, and all go down,
Let them but touch it, ev'ry one will drown;
But God remembered mercy at that hour,
The cable taughtens with a new-born pow'r,
They haul away, and from the Wreck escape,
When yet again Death seems with eager gape
To open wide his jaws,—the severed strand !
Against the fearful strain will but two stand ?
A thrill of joy passes through ev'ry heart,
They hear with ecstasy that the cut part
Is in,—but they have more to do; the mast
Is heeled anew and rigged, and thus at last,

Prepared once more to battle with the sea,
They hoist the sail, the cable cut, they're free.


With one long pealing cheer, they send to Heav'n
Bright thanks for the deliv'rance it has giv'n,
With grateful hearts, and proud they look around
On those who but for them had ne'er been found
Amongst the living; then proceed in search
Of those who have been anxious in their watch;
The Steamer for the Life-boat still looks out,
And welcomes her with long and joyous shout.
Th' 'Eclipse,' too, comes in chase, "Are her men saved?"
Three cheers they give the crew, those men who braved
And had endured so much; then comes the Smack,
Speaks them and is content, for land they tack.


The poor exhausted men the Steamer takes,
With Boat and crew in tow, for home she makes;
'Twas no light work to reach it, but at last
North Foreland, Kingsgate, Broadstairs, all are passed;

The Ramsgate pier-head light shone forth to say,
That they were welcome who had won their way
Through such a sea—it was a prosperous close—
Cheer after cheer for the brave crew arose.


The Spanish captain scarce had words to tell
How gratitude and wonder mingled well;
Pale Death had stared at him a certainty,
No boat he thought could live in such a sea.
The artist's pencil will help forth to show,
With all the glory of true feeling's glow,
How this could be and was.

      Mr. Ifold
The painting made ; in Spain hearts will turn cold
And faces pale to look at it ; but here
With pride we hail it, for we know not fear.
How can we while the British sailor lives,
And brave old England to her seamen gives
Such Boats as these ?   The trust we have is such
We tremble not,—we cannot praise too much

The Boat, or those who man her; and our thanks
Are due to those, who, foremost in the ranks
Of kindly hearts, press forward with their gold;
What if the good they do remains untold?
We do our part when we the means supply,
Else were our sailors helpless at the cry
Of shipwrecked mariner—but join the two;
Give seamen Boats,—give Bravery its due.

But while we give all honor to the brave,
And laud the Life-boat that went out to save,
Forget not the good God, without whose aid,
Vain had been ev'ry effort that was made.
At best our deeds are weak—to us is giv'n
Grace to know this—and send our thanks to Heav'n.

---

*A prose account of the Shipwreck of the "* SAMARITANO*,"*
*under the title of "* THE RAMSGATE LIFE-BOAT*," appeared*
*in "* Macmillan's Magazine*," for June 1860 ; from*
*which source this description has been taken.*

## CHARLES.

✿

AY it again—O, say once more to me
   That sweet, melodious name.   It hath a pow'r
In its full swell of sound to stir my soul,
To leave me wond'ring what hath struck its chords,
And sent so rare a music trembling home:
Repeat it to my list'ning, thirsty heart,
That drinks each letter as the droughty earth,
In hot, parched summer, sucks the falling rain;
Let it float past me toward the Spirit-world
To which it half belongs, and then come back
In eddy'ng reflux o'er my yearning brain:
Ennobled by the wreath the Angels threw,
When they turned mortal letters into pearls,
And robbed two spheres to form so rich a word.

It takes the noblest attributes of man,
And makes them patent when you say but *" Charles !"*
List! all the sweetness of the Seraphs' lyres,
In melody are chanting forth the strain ;
Hush! they are singing.  Hush—they whisper—
    *" Charles."*
Let gentle Love put in a tender word
To humanise the sound, and bring it down ;
So let it live with us within our homes,
And linger in our hearts, and on our tongues ;
The most beloved of all names under Heaven,
The sweetest, purest, noblest, and the best.

## ONE THOUGHT.

I CLAIM from thee a thought, love,
 I worship at thy shrine;
But little will content me,
 I dream not thou art mine.

Thine eye that glances from me,
 Although it gives me pain,
So noble is its movement,
 I can but look again.

My wild delirium gone,
 In which I craved thy love:
The pang I well remember,
 When speech for mast'ry strove.

Yet cold silence reigned supreme ;
  The courtesies of life
I longed, yet dared not, pay thee
  In that dread hour of strife.

My soul, while list'ning to thee,
  Was trembling lest a word
In accent should betray me—
  I'd rather die unheard.

Fire was raging in my heart,
  Yet cold as ice I seemed ;
Neglectful too you thought me—
  I was as one who dreamed.

I would have counted for thee
  My life-drops one by one,
And watched them ebbing from me—
  Glad when the last was gone.

But not for countless treasure
  Would I have had thee guess,
My heart was nestling to thee,
  Waiting for thee to bless.

Not for Golconda's riches,
  Nor California's gold,
Would I shadow forth to thee
  What must remain untold.

Yet I blush not *now* to say,
  That ever while I live,
Strong, and firm, and true to thee,
  Each beat my pulse shall give.

I love thee.   Thou art noble,
  Its impress on thy brow
Is noted well by others—
  Its presence all allow.

## One Thought.

Determined, stern, resisting,
And firm at Duty's call,
No opposition baffles,
Nor dangers thee appal.

In counting o'er thy virtues,
Love doth myself exalt;
Had I not known thy value,
This had not been my fault.

In rend'ring homage to thee,
I do but faintly show,
That solid worth sinks deeper
Than falsehood's easy flow.

Thy mantle falls upon me,
My selfishness is dead;
Hope points not to a future,
'Twas not in vain I bled.

## One Thought.

The dross has turned all golden,
   Purged by the fire of pain ;
Asking not thy love to win,
   I give thee mine again.

When thought is busy, dearest,
   A kind one wing to me ;
Dearly I buy the right, love,
   To claim as much from thee.

The keenest pang I suffer,
   Is the one racking thought,
In pain I may not soothe thee ;
   Ever to thee as naught.

I gloss the old wound over,
   My love is happy now ;
I can meet thy piercing gaze
   With fearless, open brow.

My inmost heart asks nothing
   But the burden of my song ;
One favor only grant me—
   To be remembered long.

My soul will not release thee,
   Asking but what it gives ;
The earth-born part dies slowly,
   But thought for ever lives.

## A POOR MAN'S WISH.

❁

N pale Consumption's grasp the poor man lay,
The lamp of life flickered from day to day,
And then went out in night,—and so he died.
He was a poor man, but his heart was bright,
One of the sons of toil and not well taught,
Rough on the outside ; so I scarce could tell
If I were welcome, but with gentle touch
I strove to win him to a better mind ;
And when by chance I went not for some time,
Came message, " Did it irk me much to call
And read a little to the poor sick man ? "
So from that day I knew there was a bond
Between us two, by kindly feeling wrought;

G 3

And I was proud to be the " Laborer's friend,"
As honored by his faith and trust in me,
As he was comforted when I was by.
It pained me sore to see him waste and fade,
To hear him cough, and pause between his words
Lab'ring for breath ; to see his patient air,
His silent confidence that I was grieved,
And would have spared no trouble if by aught
I could have eased him,—powerless I.
So,—nearly closed was his earth's pilgrimage
Ere to my list'ning ear he breathed the wish,
That as I had been kindly for the sake
Of One who lives above, it might be giv'n
To him, to welcome and pour forth to me
In Heav'nly regions, how he blessed my help,
And loved and honored me.

       " *In Heav'n to meet,*"—

This was the poor man's wish ; for he had come
In simple, trusting faith to look on high,
And deem his Home not built with human hands,

Nor won by any merit of his own,
Was waiting him ; and then he loved to think
That for his helper the same door stood wide,
And in some future he the welcomer.

The churchyard reached, each Sabbath-day I look
Close on my left, there lies his grass-grown grave,
That opened to receive the earth-worn part,—
The flame was quenched, and " earth to earth " dealt
     out ;
While spirit unto spirit had gone up.
'Twas if, at break of day, the waning lamp
Had sighed its last, and the pale light went forth
To mingle with the sun, and rise again
In radiant splendor.
              Oft do his words return
To urge me straightly on when I would verge
To by-paths; and at my last hour, maybe,
I shall trace back to echo of those words,
As great a debt of gratitude as he

Was pleased to pay me, if he owed it not.
He was beyond my thanks ere I knew half
The kindly thoughts and hopes he had for me,
He was so truly delicate in mind :
His weeping mother, whose bruised heart still clung
To one who had soothed *him*, this was our bond,
Oft loved to tell me how he would keep watch,
Then failing that, too weak to sit, would ask
If I were coming, and would say with warmth,
" God bless her." It is with true pleasure now
I clasp that mother's hand—she has wept sore ;
His little child went nestling to his side
Ere many months were past ; his widow once
Is wife again ; but his poor mother's heart
Will still look back, and give me smile for smile :
There's not a noble's hand the wide world through,
For which I would give up her loving clasp.

Ye who would happy be, go forth and sow,
With bounteous heart, broadcast amongst the poor,

Not scatt'ring money with a heavy hand,

Damping their honest toil,—independence,

Our common birthright, take it not away ;

But go with loving heart and tender hand,

To weep with them when grief stands at the door ;

Smile sunny smiles when they are glad with hope,

Showing respect for their own privacy ;

For no more right have we upon their hearth

Than they on ours, if they invite us not.

Sow love,—and in their hearty blessings reap

So sweet a happiness as will repay

A thousandfold to thine own world-worn self ;

For who knows not the poor are the best type

Of what our Saviour was ?   His legacy

To usward.

            'Tis as a guardian angel

In the heart, an oft-recurring strength,

To have the blessings of the loving poor

Foll'wing thy footsteps, sounding in thine ears ;

Thou canst not stray while they are looking on,

Surely thou wilt not err, when they will know
And come to doubt all goodness, if they see
The one they rev'rence falling into sin;
And more than all, thou canst not mock the dead ;
It is impossible to let them rise in judgment
Who so have left us, nothing doubting but
In Heaven they will surely welcome give :—
Not all the world from evil rails us round,
As the dead poor man's wish,—" *To meet in Heav'n.*"

## LINES ADDRESSED TO A FRIEND,

### ON THE SUDDEN DEATH BY ACCIDENT OF AN ONLY SON.

WEEP mother, weep! send forth to the dark night
A bitter cry, "Let there be no more light:"
For Nature hath reversed her own decree;
Blighted the sapling, spared the parent tree.
Now fast approaching are the feet of those
Who bring to thee one of life's keenest woes;
Did ever hour of midnight seem so wild,
So strange, so lonesome, desolate, defiled?
And yet, O gloom, continue, deepen down
To murkiest darkness, let all nature frown,
For now a mother looks on her dead son,

The fearful reign of Anguish has begun ;
The tender human voice is pow'rless here,
And agony denies her e'en a tear.
So sudden and so fearful was his end,
They could not even murmur " God defend !"
For ere the thought of danger could arise,
His soul had winged its flight beyond the skies ;
And the poor empty casket home they bring,
God! how the sight his parents' hearts must wring !
Was there no ministering Angel near,
Who could have saved a life to them so dear ;
If only to have sent him safely home,
That he might wither gently to the tomb ?
Of all the hosts that Heav'n retains, not one :
And so he died.   A loved, an only son !


\*        \*        \*        \*        \*


In the calm summer night, toll forth, O bell,
With a sharp sudden clangor, a death-knell ;

Float past us on the air, return again
And moan, as one who writhes in mortal pain ;
Ring out a fierce note for a bitter woe,
Muffle thy tone, weep now in accents low ;
In turn be tender and be harsh in turn,
The varied moods of a great sorrow learn ;
And as a thing of life, proclaim aloud
With mournful voice, " They wrap him in his shroud."
Lament, O bell, ever lament his fate,
Strike into human hearts, as if in hate,
A dagger sharp and keen; so let them know
By sudden intuition, that a blow
But seldom equalled in our careworn world,
Has on two Parents' hearts this night been hurled.
Ring till thy notes grow hoarse with grief and pain,
Stay not to measure out what they contain,
But send them forth unthinking ; let us hear
Confusion wild, distress, and nervous fear.
Then give Monotony her long, dull reign,
Rock in her arms her fretful sister, Pain ;

And let the air vibrate for miles around,
With the same mournful, dreary, heaving sound ;
'Twill echo in sad hearts for many years,
And be repaid thee well in falling tears.


\*        \*        \*        \*        \*


Sad Mother! never yet upon this earth,
In any tongue, has language given birth
To words of comfort for a grief like thine,
Or I would study it and make them mine ;
The will to do it only I possess,
And panting sympathy makes small pow'r less,
Takes from me what lies trembling on my tongue,
Leaves me a throbbing heart, but words, not one.
I seem to look upon thy deep'ning grief aghast,
As one who trembles at the tempest's blast,
And with prophetic vision sees afar
How its wild fury unrestrained will mar,
And desolation grasp with eager hand

The goodly vessel lab'ring on the strand,
Making a total wreck.   What is it to thee,
That the bright sun sporting makes jubilee?
'Twill never bring *his* shadow to the Hall,
Its summer beam can only gild his pall.
The calm smile of the soft and silv'ry moon,
Can bring to thy tired heart no greater boon
Than that it bore to him.
                           For evermore,
Lone Mother, ever and for evermore,
Sorrow hath cast her cankered meshes round thee:
In vain appeal to Time, no helper he;
Thy troubled aspect he will make more calm,
And thoughtless tongues will say, "He brought thee
          balm
Upon his healing wings," but I say, "No,"
He never yet assuaged a *real woe;*
He'll sink it deep and deeper down, each day
Instead of weak'ning, strengthening its sway;
To sight of others lost, never to thine,

Hiding as darkness hides within the mine.
But is the ship less lost because each wave
Sinking her lower, makes our power to save
Less and still less, till the insidious sand
Closes around her its relentless hand;
Its myriad fingers clasping round her form,
As though with care to shield her from the storm:
Is she less lost, I ask, because she lies
Engulphed in changing quicksands from our eyes?
And shall we say we have outlived our grief,
Because, despairing to receive relief,
We bury out of sight of human eye
Our lost, wrecked happiness, our misery?

\*        \*        \*        \*        \*

Calm, calm, a long, dark, silent, weary calm,
A dreary nothingness, nor good, nor harm,
Come near us with a living homely touch,

The deep despair and aching gnaw are such
We cannot feel, life is no longer life ;
Our shudd'ring heart declines the farther strife.
It has closed over the fell wound, and left
Existence blank, of all its flow'rs bereft.
Poor panting, struggling, pang-torn, human heart!
Will no one to the rescue come, and part
Thy woe with thee, too great to bear alone ?
See with what grace descending from a throne
Comes the All-pitying, in our hour of need
His tender hand soweth immortal seed.
Low fall at his dear feet and bruisèd be,
Lest past thine hour of choice He fall on thee ;
A crushing fall, a stony, fearful weight,
Who ever lived and looked upon his hate ?
Who ever looked Him back his love again,
And was not eased of more than half their pain ?
His heart divine, yet human, understands
What eager suff'ring looks for from his hands :

The great physician He, appeal to Him,
And when thy cup of woe fills to the brim,
He'll take it gently from thy trembling palm,
Staunch the fresh wound, pouring in oil and balm.
And is it full, dear friend, thy cup of woe?
Indeed, I marvel not thou thinkest so;
Each in his own sorrow sadly seeing
How warped and tangled is his thread of being,
Waiting the day when all will be made clear—
Thinks, " Surely, *I'm* the greatest suff'rer here,"
And knows not many a familiar face,
Casting aside the veil, would take his place,
And gladly 'scape the cold and chilling blight,
Which makes his seeming joy one long, dark night.

Ah! weeping Mother, bitter is the cup
Thy trembling lip refuseth to drink úp;
But other cups there are of larger size,
Which have been spared thy tear-dimmed, aching eyes:

God's own hand took him, not a stranger blow
Struck at him in the dark, felling him low ;
No dastard hand uplifted took his life,
Nor perished he by friend in mortal strife,
Nor did he wilfully his soul set free :
An angel whispered " God hath need of thee."
O Mother ! comfort take. We all must weep
And sorrow, that he sleeps unwaking sleep ;
We weep for thee, and thou for him. Weep on !
Let fall the flowing tear for one that's gone ;
Yet when they cease, that dull, void, voiceless pain,
We hoped we had escaped from, comes again
And bides with us.
            " Father, thy will be done,"
Thou seest by what martyrdom is won
The strength to *feel* these words,—we strive to see,
While quiv'ring from the stroke, thy kind " need be."
Pity our darkened vision as we kneel,
Praying to feel no more the probing steel.

                                H

And to these sorrowing Parents ever send
Such comfort as most heavenward shall tend ;
As to the tomb they take their destined way,
May " strength be granted equal to their day."

## SONG OF THE BLIND GIRL.

※

A H ! my poor heart, and why so sad,
   Whence do these mists arise ?
Why must thou look on happiness,
   Ever through others' eyes ?

Blind, blind, alas ! they little know,
   Who have the gift of sight,
That when they say, " How beautiful ! "
   I feel my long dark night.

And wonder why some things they call
   Fair and of roseate hue ;
In vain they speak of colors bright,
   Dark crimson, purple, blue.

H 3

Hot tears lie trembling in my heart
    But rise not to mine eye ;
Poor darkened orb ! in vain I raise
    It, sightless to the sky.

"Never to look upon a friend,"
    This is my meed of woe :
My fingers glide their face across,
    Touch sensitive and slow.

Be still, sad heart ! the shadow rests
    With heavy, drooping wing ;
And never will its blight depart,
    Until in heaven I sing.

✠

## "GARIBALDI FOR EVER."

FOR ever? "Garibaldi for ever!"
So shout the people, and the English heart
Becomes an echo to the merry chime
Rung out by fair Italia's wak'ning life.
Go on, Deliv'rer! ev'ry noble beat
Of thy great heart, is bringing free-born health
To worst of slaves, is striking off the print
Of mind-worn fetters, deadliest of all.—
Time dies at thine approach—Eternity,
That only can embrace thee, stretcheth forth
Caressing—with, "For ever, O my son."
Joseph, the youngest born, upon thy brow
The vastness of its might has settled down;

And may the hand-writing, unseen by all
Save thine own glorious self, now guide thee on.
" Garibaldi for ever ! "   Ever on,
Noblest of nature's nobles, who ne'er errs
In crowning.   Kingliest of kingly men,
Exhaust we all the epithets e'er coined
In lavish haste, we yet must miss the word
That could enrich thee aught, for thou hast won,
By force of thine own worth, a better crown
Than Earth can gem from out her hidden hoards ;
The wealth and title of a King would take,
From off thine honored brow, its brightest wreath
And make thee poor indeed—in spirit poor ;
Thou who art now so rich !   For thine own love
Of liberty and nobleness, a wealth
That drops not from thee in a lowly state :
Then add to that the blessings of thy race,
To whom the name of GARIBALDI stands,
When they would speak of honor, virtue, fame,
Or love of country, bravery, and all

That dignifies, ennobles, elevates,
And renders godlike.  A world-wide hero
Thou, while history holds its course,—thine Empire,
The countless millions who shall people earth,
To bless the man who freed them from their chains,
While they bear on the echo to its goal,
The rising generations; and the words
In never-ending cycles rise around :—
" For ever! Garibaldi for ever ! "

## KINGCUPS AND DAISIES.

⁘

THE kingcups are flow'ring around thee,
   Glistening with golden sheen;
But they gild not the daylight to me, love,
   They but brighten the grass so green.
        In vain they hold
        Their cups of gold,
      To one whose thirst is slaked.


The daisies are blossoming near thee,
   Eyes of gold in silver set;
But they win not a smile from my lip, love,
   They but spangle the grass so wet.
        In vain they hold,
        Silver and gold,
      To one whose eye is closed.

My tear-drops are falling upon thee,
　　Bedewing thine early grave;
But they give no fresh life to thy heart, love,
　　They but show that they could not save.
　　　　　　In vain they fall,
　　　　　　Bitter as gall,
　　　　　For one whose life has fled.


My heart is with'ring, breaking for thee,
　　Bursting with groans in anguish deep;
But its life-throbs reach not to thine ear, love,
　　They but rock thee to sounder sleep.
　　　　　　In vain I lie,
　　　　　　With bitter cry,
　　　　　By one whose ear is sealed.


The kingcup of gold, the daisy bright,
　　That close round my failing heart,

But blossom and fall in weariness, love,
They but whisper my soul, "Depart."
So fading here,
They'll come next year,
Finding a two-fold grave.

## TO MY ANONYME.

❀

HE winds have answered thee, O noble Bard!
  The birds have thy behest obeyed;
And flow'rs of rarest beauty at thy call,
  Around my head in wreaths have swayed.

The softest breathings of a first young love,
  As murm'rings of the mild south wind,
Roved o'er my cheek as ye invoked the spell,
  Leaving a tell-tale blush behind.

A bird came as from Paradise to me,
  And sang, methinks, as sweet a song
As e'er to mortal ears was warbled forth,—
  My mem'ry doth its notes prolong.

Fresh perfumed flow'rs in wild profusion sprung,
　E'en as I read the blissful call,
That was to place them on my aching brow,
　From which that wreath shall never fall.


Thy wishes bore fruition as thy pen
　Traced them on paper, for to me
Their sweetness brought, on fancy's gilded wing,
　All that of happiness can be.


And for the last sad chord upon thy lyre,
　That would have others mourn me dead;
Enough, sweet poet! if *thou* shouldst lament
　When my last spark of life has fled.

## MY DOG "FEARLESS."

❂

NONE love me as I once was loved,
   My faithful dog to me
Gave, what no living mortal could,
   Unwav'ring constancy.

His wild free glance that dared defy,
   While at his truant play,
Would oft return my leave to ask,
   Waiting the words, " You may."

Would almost disobey to hear
   My voice raised in command,
And then droop low with bashful mien,
   In full obedience stand.

My pretty one, it irks me now,
  That I must walk alone;
The tears well up to think that thou
  Art to the dark grave gone.

Thou wert so lightsome and so free,
  With such an endless grace,
So ever new and yet the same,
  Of weariness no trace.

Thine eye was Beauty's bright-born self,
  As seeking to meet mine,
Thy brown orbs sent such rays of love,—
  'Tis for that love I pine.

Yet bright and piercing as they were,
  Sure thou wert very blind;
My goodness quick enough to see,
  My faults were cast behind.

And if I grieved,—then nestling close,
    So tender and so true—
Thy gentle tongue would lick my hand,
    And fondle it anew.

The turf is green above thee now,
    And winter's cold white snow
Has fall'n and melted oftentimes,
    Since my hand laid thee low.

And often have I thought to pen
    The love I bear to thee,
As often have I failed, because
    For tears I could not see.

No other dog thy place supplies;
    I mock not my own heart
With a vain semblance, that would be
    At ev'ry turn a dart,

To stab and rankle and remind,
   How great my loss in thee ;
I need not prompting, O my dog,
   Oft it recurs to me.

I would give many treasures that
   Are precious in my sight,
To have thee gambol at my side,
   In ever fresh delight.

Thy long hair streaming in the wind,
   Thy pace almost as fleet,
When my voice urged thine onward path,
   Or thou hadst come to greet ;

When on return from visit long,
   Thou wouldst from far espy
Her who was all the world to thee ;
   Then almost thou didst fly.

O " Fearless" thou hadst many names:
" Dog-fiend," and many more ;
But 'twas in love I called thee so,
From out my boundless store.

And thou didst understand me too,
We knew each other well ;
If I had fault thou wouldst not see,
If thou,—I will not tell.

Our bond remains unbroken still,
Each to the other true ;
Our grief and love together blend,
As ivy on a yew.

I loved thee for thyself alone,
And thou didst make to me
Return so ample, that thy loss
Can ne'er replacèd be.

I

My own hand wrapped thee in thy shroud,
    And lowered thee to bed ;
And for each tear that I have dropt,
    A daisy lifts its head.

And they are tipt of carmine hue,
    In very truth they know
What mingled with the falling show'r,
    For him who slept below.

O Cynic—have I said too much?
    'Tis but *my dog* I weep;
And is it bitter in thy mouth,
    That so fond watch I keep?

Then my offence is done.  For thou
    Canst join in my reply;
" Show me two mortals who have loved,
    As did my dog and I."

# LOVE.

❊

LOVE—O Love—coming with step so gentle,
  Thy gracious feet bathed in the morning dew,
To my hot heart as the large drops of rain,
  Which summer sheds from Heav'n's mystic blue
To the parched earth.  Sweeter art thou to me
Than is the bean-made honey to the bee.

My being shadows forth a nobler end,
  As thy warm breath, O Love, darts through my soul;
Like nature wak'ning at the touch of spring
  I trembling lie, yielding to thy control.
O whisp'ring Love, more sweet art thou to me
Than music sighing o'er a moonlit sea.

I 3

Bide with me, gentle Love, go not away;
  Dark would the world be shouldst thou leave me now,
For ev'ry bright'ning hue which thou hast shed,
  Would deepen into shadow on my brow.
Go not away—dearer art thou to me
Than prattl'ng childhood on its parent's knee.

Sweet wand'rer, though I asked thee not to come,
  Yet thou art welcome, as the sun at noon
To dungeon captive,—willing slave am I;
  Hugging my chains, craving no greater boon
Than to be thine.   For dearer thou to me
Than fairest penitent at priestly knee.

Ay—think not we will part—an' thou must go,
  I take my trav'lling staff and with thee start,
By mountain, hill, and vale I follow thee,
  The world's Sahara powerless to part;
Better to journey, O sweet Love, with thee
In painful toil, than separate to be.

Rather than live without thee, gentle Love—
    Infatuated, I would follow on,
Till, failing thy swift footsteps to o'ertake,
    I e'en must sink, still blessing thee alone,—
One 'mongst the many martyrs that have bled for thee—
When dies the last, ends the world's history.

## TO EMMA R.

※

NOT when the adulation of the world
    Is hov'ring round thee, and uplifted praise
With myriad tongues is chanting forth thy name,
Can I come near thee ; I am backward then,
I fall behind and seem no more a friend :
I sit beside thee silent and abashed,
To *feel* what others can so glibly *say.*
My swelling heart can coin no words to tell
How one emotion fights another down,
And all is chaos as I look and love.
Yet have I often thought thine eye hath seen
And noted, in my kindling mien, the flame
That dieth never. Yes, it hath whispered me,
That 'mongst the babbling of the silver-tongued,

And far beyond their loudest trump of praise,
E'en higher than their widest flights of speech,
The silence of my soul hath reached to thine,
And the mute stricken one who had no words
Spoke in a language more akin to thee,
Striking a deeper chord more pure and clear.
Only when others, jesting, dare to say
Aught in dispraise, can I uplift my voice ;
Then from the quiver of my rankling heart,
I take the keenest arrow ever winged
And send it twanging from the bended bow,
To see them bleeding, wounded unto death,
At feet of her who laughs to see their pain.
Bright Emma ! there are depths within thine eye
Unfathomed by my wistful, tender gaze,
Eluding ever as I think I grasp ;
While clutching at thy thoughts I drowning, sink,
Down, down, into the troubled waters, where
A dark uncertainty flows over all.
I cannot reach thee, but I sit and wait

With mournful patience, I abide my time,
I smile my anguish back into my heart
While watching for the boon that may not come,
And wildly, vainly yearning for thy love.
But now in midnight hour while others sleep,
I lift my voice and weeping call to thee;
What I have stifled when I feared thy glance
By Heav'n's messenger I send.   Oh! see,
It is a costly gift, a human heart.
They come not often flutt'ring to our feet,
Even to thine, not *often*, O my friend!
An' if thou wilt reject it, say but so,
And I will slay it as it kneels to thee;
Will kill the better part, its hopes and fears,
Making but one vast dreamless, dreary tomb,
Where thou mayst walk for hours, yet never find
One blooming flow'r to gather to thy hand.
The time has come when thou canst make a choice,
It passes by thee into the endless space,
For losing once the thread, thou wilt not find

The subtle clue by which to lure it back;
Evading one who meted out but scorn,
Or meaner still, a cold indifference,
For such a wealth of love, as should have rung
A heaven-made echo in thy spirit's home.
Praise thee as others do?   No, not for worlds.
Why vaunt the diamond?   Why tell pure gold
It is not dross?   Why gather up sweet pearls
Babbling their beauty?   Or the precious stones,
Saying, " They are not glass ?"   And why of thee
Pour forth vain words that cannot even tell
One tithe of the rich treasures of thy brain,
Or semble in the faintest type to me
Thyself, with all thy bright belongings?
Perish the pen that so could mar thy worth,
Or think to model crown for thee, when Heaven
Sent down its best,—NATURE'S NOBILITY.

## TO CHARLES WESTERTON.

[*Written October 1859, during his one year's respite from the Church-wardenship of St. Paul's, Knightsbridge.*]

CHARLES WESTERTON! it is a name beloved,
And all true hearts leap to the sound of it;
A warrior leaning on his sword awhile,
A mariner at rest upon his oars;
But as the war-horse champing on the bit,
His spirit urges to the conflict still.
And he will not be wanting, when the fight
Is hottest, fiercest,—you will find him there.
True Englishman, stout Protestant, brave heart!
An honor to thy Country and thy Church,
We know thou dost but bide a fitting time
To be what thou hast been, the foe of those

Who would our freedom crush, and bow our necks
Beneath a tyranny, that takes its root
In basest falsehood, and bears poison-flowers.
Watch by us, good old friend! we look to thee,
Our champion thou, stand by us to the last,
And we will back thee 'gainst thine enemies.
The Nation's cause is thine, and anxious eyes
Look on thee, hearts are list'ning for thy voice.
Thou hast braved much, and yet we ask for more ;
Thy giant soul will answer to the call.
Already on thy brow the victor's wreath,
(For England placed it there,) but not his rest.
Again we urge thee to the battle field,
Though bloodless ; yet not all the hounds of war,
If banded to one spot, could equal those
Who track thy footsteps, their *hate* spurred by *fear*.
God guide, God guard, God speed thee on thy way,
And may the star that in the *East* arose,
Descend on thee, " Time-honored WESTERTON."

## TO CHARLES WESTERTON,

*[As eight years Churchwarden of St. Paul's, Knightsbridge, calling upon him, after a lapse of but one year, to resume his arduous duties in defence of the Non-Confessional Church of England against her aggressors, on Easter Tuesday, 1860.]*

✻

AWAKE! brave friend, there is no rest for thee,
　Toil on strong heart, fierce will the conflict be;
Now in the hour of need with firm, clear tone,
Comes a united call for "WESTERTON!"
God wots of all things: we can only guess
The stern hard strife, the utter weariness
To which we summon thee; yet not a doubt
Of failure mars the triumph of the shout.
He comes and who will second him? "All, all,"
*Our cause is his*, with him we stand or fall.
Are his hands weak? We press to bear them up.

Is the draught bitter ?   We will share the cup.

Come to his aid all ye who love the right,

Ere the dark shadow of a cowl-black night

Fall on us.   See, he grapples for dear life,

Support *him* lest *we* perish in the strife.

We called him to his post, and now he turns

Looking on us; within his eye there burns

The martyr's light.   Woe to us if we shrink

Or idly waver, standing on the brink

Of so dark future, that I fear to tell

What his keen glance has fathomed but too well.

Look on us, Friend.   We are no dastard crew,

Our hearts are of good metal, they ring true;

The air is heavy with the tramping of our feet;

Our name is Legion, we have come to meet

Oppression, Ignorance, and Priestly Pride,

With other nameless evils, side by side.

We quail not, looking on thy manly face,

We feel the right man stands in the right place.

Retracing all the worn-out past, we say,

" *He* bore the heat and burden of the day ;"
The pregnant future facing us with stare
Of ghastly import, " You will find *him* there,"
We say with cheery voice, and off we go
To our day's toil ; to thee we leave the foe.
What shall thy guerdon be ?   A nation's love,
A murmuring that shall echo from above,
And vibrate as each generation comes,
A " household word " in all our happy homes.
The old, the young, the brave, the faint of heart,
Will mingle voices, " Well he bore his part
For us the people.   Ah ! 'twas nobly done,
No name so dear to us as WESTERTON !"

LONDON:

PRINTED BY GEORGE PHIPPS, 13 & 14, TOTHILL STREET,

WESTMINSTER.

# NEW WORKS
# PUBLISHED BY MR. WESTERTON.

## NOTICE TO AUTHORS.—MSS. FOR PUBLICATION.

Authors of Original Biographies, Histories of Periods or Places, Narratives of Personal Adventures by Sea or Land, or any works in Divinity or General Literature, should send their MSS to Mr. WESTERTON, who, if they are approved of, will forward the Terms on which he will undertake their publication.

## I.

*Now Ready, in One Vol., Price Half-a-Guinea.*

# New Relations, and Bachelor's Hall.

### By URBIN RUS.

"Intended to illustrate the evils of gambling and extravagance, these two Tales display considerable talent; they are eminently interesting. The author is able to construct an exciting story, and vividly to delineate character."—*Illustrated News of the World.*

"We cannot but be struck with the evidences of inventive power which they exhibit; and we should be glad if our hurried glance at them should tend to introduce them to the notice of our numerous readers."—*Illustrated London News.*

## II.

*Now Ready, Two Vols, price One Guinea,*

# Rocks and Shoals.

### By CAPT. LOVESY.

"Event succeeds event in a highly effective and dramatic manner. An amusing and well-constructed story, varied in its incidents, smart in its style, and unflagging in its interest."—*Daily Telegraph.*

"Under the above title, Captain Lovesy has produced a most agreeable work. The reflection, judgment, and moral axioms which run through many of the pages are highly creditable to the writer. To those who wish to enjoy a hearty laugh, or shed a tear over the sorrows of a Magdalen, we strongly recommend the volumes under notice. They will amply repay a perusal."—*The Review.*

"ROCKS AND SHOALS may have a moral object, or it may not. It certainly is a moral homily in its way, if rightly read; but it is somewhat more to the purpose than a moral fiction (that contradiction in terms); *for it is a most amusing, a most original, and most pleasing novel; under these circumstances, it will not want for readers.*"—*The Observer.*

"A very effective though highly coloured picture of a certain class of life, and of a nature which will always have peculiar attractions to those who devour light literature. A single quotation, the very life-like description of the firm of Dodgeley and Hawker, will give a very sufficient, and, we believe, a very favourable idea of Captain Lovesy's style."—*The Critic.*

"The events succeed each other with a dramatic rapidity which interests and drags the reader on to the conclusion."

"The reader will find himself insensibly interested in his story, which is simple, amusing, and replete with incident."—*Morning Chronicle.*

"This is a capital book; and should *Rocks and Shoals* really be his first work, we are inclined to regard him as a male Minerva of fiction, sprung from the head of an imaginative Jove. A vein of quiet and caustic wit, an intimate acquaintance with the world and its ways, and a never-failing current of sound philosophical thought pervade the whole book, and we care not how soon we may be called upon to sit in judgment upon another from the same hand. The adventures of Mr. Geoffrey Hibblethwaite, the hero, are amusing in the extreme, and act as an admirable frame-work to no inconsiderable amount of sly humour and genial good feeling; nor have we read half-a-dozen pages ere we begin to accord to him alike our confidence and our sympathy."

"We have indulged somewhat largely in extracts, and can afford no further space than is required to assure our readers that the loss will be their own, should they not also become those of Captain Lovesy, to whom we offer a cordial *au revoir.*"—*Literary Gazette.*

III.

*In Two Vols., price One Guinea,*

# The Morning of Life.

## By the Author of " GORDON OF DUNCAIRN."

" The promise which *Gordon of Duncairn* gave that its gifted Author would one day rise to eminence in this walk of literature, appears to be abundantly confirmed in the delightful Volumes before us, abounding with incidents supplied from the ever-flowing fountain of human life, and endowed with a freshness and originality all their own, while the sentiments attributed to the leading personages in the little drama which they describe, bespeak qualities both of the mind and of the heart of a *high* order of refinement."—*Morning Advertiser.*

" The first volume of this work traces the development of the passion of love in a poor girl, from her tenderest years up to the period of early womanhood, when it manifests itself in its full vigour; the second subjects her to those trials and reverses which test the purity of her affection, and finally crown it with supreme triumph.

" The blossoming of the young girl's affections is beautifully painted; every shadow that darkens her pure mind, as well as every gleam of sunshine that lightens and warms it, are hit off with a truth and distinctness which are little less than marvellous. Even the oldest and most withered of us must, in reading this charming record, be sensible of that 'one touch of nature which makes the whole world kin.' We give the author unqualified praise for the originality of her design, and for the masterly skill with which she has carried it into execution. We say *she*, for assuredly the Author is a woman; no man's hand could ever yet have touched the affections with so much delicacy and truth. We lay down the *Morning of Life* with sincere admiration for the Author's powers, and with an estimate no less high of her moral qualifications to be a teacher of what is wise and true under the fascinating guise of fiction."—*Illustrated News of the World.*

" There are many to whom it will be a very great favorite; and there are many scenes in it that are composed with great skill."—*Critic.*

" *The Morning of Life* is a novel of what must be designated the "sensational ' class, in contradistinction to the novel of incident and action, depending as it does for its principal effect upon the milder form of mental emotion. It purports to be the autobiography of a young intelligent girl, the second daughter of a country clergyman; and it professes to give an account of all the hopes and fears that kindle hop—all the sentiments, feelings, and anticipations of the pseudo author from childhood, or rather the age of reason which succeeds childhood, to the hour of marriage."

" *The Morning of Life* is an exceedingly pleasing novel, well written, and bound ing in just sentiments elegantly expressed."—*Observer.*

---

IV.

*In One Vol., price Half-a-Guinea.*

# Shadow and Sunshine;
## Or, THE TWO COUSINS.

## By MAUUICE KEITH.

" Omne tulit punctum, qui miscuit utile dulci."—Hor.

" The story is much more dramatic than the reader might be led to expect from a perusal of the earlier pages; and the author's description of persons and places, an escenes at home and abroad are well sustained, while the moral is sound to the core."—*Morning Advertiser.*

" The personal mechanism of the work is uncommonly well sustained, and the sentiments placed in the lips of the dominant characters are sound and good. —*Illustrated News of the World.*

" We have only one fault to find with *Shadow and Sunshine*, and that is, that it is too short, for the story is told in a single volume. The story is well told, the characters are ably drawn, and the language is forcible. It reflects the highest credit on the Author, who will be certain to reap a large amount of approbation." —*Review.*

"The various characters are well sketched and grouped; and in saying we have perused Mr. Keith's novel with considerable pleasure, we feel confident that its readers generally will be inspired with a similar sentiment. Works of this description rise superior to the ordinary flimsy literature of the day, and by enchaining the attention to an interesting story, unobtrusively inculcate many valuable truths and sentiments, which may take po-session of the mind of a casual reader and lead him effectually to reflection on subjects less attractively treated in a purely didactic treatise."—*National Standard.*

---

### V.

*In One Vol., price Five Shillings.*

# Pilgrim Walks,

## A CHAPLET OF MEMORIES.

## By Mrs. ROBERT CARTWRIGHT.

Among other places visited and described are—The Cathedrals of Canterbury, Chichester, Salisbury, Exeter, and Amiens ; Rufus's Stone, Stonehenge, Château de Versailles, and The Château d'Eu.

"Mrs. Robert Cartwright writes like an accomplished English Lady, with excellent feeling and intelligence."—*Daily News.*

"Mrs. Robert Cartwright has added to her reputation by this new production of her graceful pen. The volume consists of a series of finished sketches, delineating some of the most interesting public monuments at home and abroad, and all displaying quickness of apprehension, with soundness of judgment and exquisite taste. Her acute and brilliant criticism on architecture, statuary, and painting, gives an enhanced value to her charms of description, and renders the book not only entertaining but instructive. We have seldom met so much attractive matter within so small a compass."—*National Standard.*

---

### VI.

*In Two Vols., price One Guinea.*

# The Wife's Temptation ;

## A STORY OF BELGRAVIA.

## By MRS. CHALLICE,

Author of " The Sister of Charity," " The Laurel and the Palm," &c.

"The Novel of the Season."—*Morning Advertiser.*

"All that there is of noble, self-sacrificing, and hopeful in woman finds a warm and eloquent advocate in the pen that wrote these pages."—*Morning Post.*

"For its stirring interest and loftiness of purpose, one of the best novels ever read."—*Sunday Times.*

"It brings us face to face with things and people as they are. It is embellished with keen wit, subtle satire, and the deepest pathos."—*Civil Service Gazette.*

"The remarkable nature of some of the personages imparts a brilliancy and vigour to the story, which combines a good purpose with the attractions of an interesting fiction."—*The Sun.*

"Supremely eminent in vigour, and must command our earnest attention."—*South London Times.*

"The tale is one of thrilling agonizing interest, written with great freedom, spirit, and power."—*Caledonian Mercury.*

"Replete in its development with womanly tenderness."—*Weekly Dispatch.*

"We congratulate the authoress upon having gained this high literary prize."—*The Review.*

"Not unworthy the fertile brain of Dumas."—*The Critic.*

"The many characters which are introduced, and the animated scenes wherein they figure, denote a close observation of life."—*News of the World.*

VII.

*In One Vol., price 10s. 6d.*

# Luxima, the Prophetess;
## A TALE OF INDIA.

### By LADY MORGAN.

" Most powerfully drawn and the untimely fate of both gives a deep interest to the conclusion of the tale."—*Morning Advertiser.*

" The unvarying phases of the Eastern character, superstitions and customs, impart to this novel an ever-enduring freshness. The story is one of exceeding interest, and will be much admired by the lovers of the romantic and the sentimental."—*Sunday Times.*

" It is one of the best works of its class."—*Morning Chronicle.*

" Powerfully drawn."—*Illustrated London News.*

" There is much imagination in the scenes of the story and luxuriance of description; one of the best specimens of a literature which nevertheless exercised too great an influence on its age and country to be forgotten."—*New Quarterly Review.*

" There is a picturesque freshness about some of its descriptions, which would not be easy to excel."— *Critic.*

" A charming tale."—*Weekly Dispatch.*

" Replete with soul-stirring incident and deep interest."—*Country Gentleman's Journal.*

" It is interesting as having been one of the earliest productions of the lamented authoress, and the *very latest on which her pen was employed before her death.*"—*The Critic.*

---

VIII.

*In One Volume, price Half-a-Crown.*

# Emily Morton; a Tale.
## WITH SKETCHES FROM LIFE AND CRITICAL ESSAYS.

*Contents :*

SIR E. BULWER LYTTON'S PRINCIPLES OF ART IN FICTION.
A LECTURE ON POETRY.
THE SHAM FIGHT IN HYDE PARK.
CAPTAIN ACKERLEY'S LECTURE IN ST. JAMES'S PARK.

### By CHARLES WESTERTON.

" A little, but a good book. We have very seldom perused a pocket volume of miscellaneous matter more interesting and entertaining, from the simplicity of style and graphic power with which the several subjects are treated. In the tale of " Emily Morton" the author displays a power of pathos and effective delineation of character, which impress us with the conviction that, were he to devote his pen to novel writing, he would rank among our most favourite authors. Its appearance some years since in a periodical of the day, elicited the marked approbation of one of the justest and acutest of literary critics—the late Charles Ollier ; whose favourable report of any production was a sure stamp of its excellence."—*National Standard.*

" A novelette by Mr. Westerton is an unlooked-for fact. It is interesting to mark that the principles which have led to Mr. Westerton's notoriety, were his fixed guides years back. Mr. Westerton's book is thoroughly healthy and English throughout."—*Literary Gazette.*

" Mr. Westerton is willing enough to show how books should be written as well as published, and in this little volume makes a fair enough demonstration of talent. The leading tale is simple and obvious, but pathetic in treatment and sentiment. Among the critical essays is one on 'Sir B. Lytton and his Principles of Art in Fiction,' which is argued with considerable acumen, if not always with accuracy."—*The Leader.*

" Of the other papers, ' Captain Ackerley's Lectures in St. James' Park,' in which that eccentric individual with his ' Lamp of Glory ' is capitally described, holding forth to a motley audience ; and ' A Sham Fight in Hyde Park,' are highly humourous sketches. ' A Lecture on Poetry,' delivered at the City of London Mechanics' Institution, and an extremely sound and well-written article on ' Sir Edward Bulwer Lytton and his Principles of Art in fiction,' complete the volume. Mr. Westerton has done well in presenting these few effusions of his leisure in a collected form. He will do even better to resume the pen which he wields with facility and skill, and add the laurels of authorship to his other deserved claims upon public estimation."—*National Standard,* July 2.

" Mr. Westerton has shown nearly as much strong sense in this book, as he has manifested in his political conduct. His purpose is earnest, and his manner of fulfilling that purpose highly creditable to his natural talents."—*Bell's Messenger.*

## IX.

*Third Edition, 2 vols. price 12s.*

# Italy and Her Revolution in 1831,

## BEING THE ADVENTURES OF CASTELLAMONTE.

### By ANTONIO GALLENGA, Member of the Sardinian Legislature.

Author of " The History of Piedmont," " Italy in 1848," " Fra Dolcino," " Country Life in Piedmont," &c.

" M. Gallenga writes with the feelings, tastes, experience and knowledge of an Englishman ; but on writing of Italy he writes of his native country. He has an independent mind, sound judgment, and plenty of common sense."—*Saturday Review.*

" Castellamonte is excellent ; few fictions are equal to it in mournful excitement."—*Westminster Review.*

" Signor Castellamonte has a good deal to say, and an amusing way of saying it. A good deal of zest is given to the narrative from first to last, by the introduction, in the midst of highly coloured and exciting pages, of ironical touches and grotesque reflections which leave the reader, for a moment, in doubt, whether the whole is not intended as a satire. . . . The scenes among students, their bombastic proposals, the ludicrous incongruity of their ideas, their open-air conspiracy are here painted admirably. . . . The ride to Reggio, the encounter with the priest, and the mad race back are related in a lively manner. . . . The author contrives to keep us, from beginning to end of his narrative, in a state of cheerful vivacity."—*Athenæum, Feb.* 4.

" One of the most instructive and amusing works of the season. The Daguerreotype of Life in Italy."—*Britannia, Feb.* 18.

" An historical romance of the time of the Revolution of 1831. A striking picture of the revolutionary period."—*Literary Gazette, Feb.* 18.

" In these well-written and highly interesting volumes, a graphic sketch is presented to us of a great number of startling incidents which marked the progress of the great movement to which they refer, and they convey, at the same time, an idea by no means exaggerated of the lofty sentiments, noble self devotion and adventurous daring of Italian patriotism. Its pages are deeply characterised by an attachment to Italy—a desire which no reverse can damp of seeing her one day triumph over foreign thraldom, and a confidence alike in the justice of her cause and the worthiness of her people, which sustains the hope of her ultimate success. . . . Among the numerous stories with which the book abounds, that entitled ' Catching a Bishop,' is extremely entertaining. The incident is uncommonly well told. . . . The book will well repay the trouble of reading on historical considerations, whilst its literary merits are sufficient to recommend it to the higher classes of English readers."—*Morning Advertiser, January* 25.

" In the narrative itself there is great variety of incident, and the scenes in the state prison at Conegiano, the skirmish at Forenzola, the capture of the Bishop of Guastalla, the watch at the city gate, and lastly the escape of the author out of the power of the Austrian soldiers, are told with great vivacity and effect."—*Morning Post.*

" Alas, poor Italy ! Twice has hope towered up to the sky ; twice was it dashed to the ground. Must we resign it ? Oh ! who would not die that Italy may live !"—*Author's Farewell.*

## THE LATE GENERAL SIR WILLIAM NAPIER.

The death of a good soldier and a great historian cannot be allowed to pass without special record. Had William Francis Patrick Napier been simply a titled survivor of the Peninsular war, he would have figured with some note in the obituary of the year, but his service in the field, gallant as it was, has been eclipsed by his labours in the study, and he now stands, and will stand for ages, in the eyes of his countrymen, as the chronicler of their country's greatest exploits.

The supremacy of Napier's *History* soon became incontestable. The truth is, besides the genuine nationality of its object and its tone, there was a dignity in the treatment and a living verity in the descriptions which led the mind unresistingly captive. Never before had such scenes been portrayed, nor with such wonderful colouring. As event after event was unfolded in the panorama, not only the divisions and the brigades, but the very regiments and regimental officers of the Peninsular army became familiarized to the public eye. Marches, combats, and battles came out upon the canvass with the fidelity of photographs, while the touches by which the effect was produced bespoke, not the ingenuities of historic art, but the involuntary suggestions of actual memory. The shrillness of Crawfurd's scream at Busaco as he ordered the Light Division to charge, was probably ringing in the author's ears as he wrote; and the whole scene upon the Coa, with the little drummer-boy beating the charge, the French officer, " in a splendid uniform," leaping on the bridge, and the surgeon tending the wounded in the midst of the fire, must have risen before his eyes as he drew it. For the sake of painting like this,—for the sake of an eloquence unknown before, and devoted unreservedly to the recompense of British valour, people readily forgave the prepossessions or deficiencies of the work. When the magnificence of its diction culminated into sublimity in the stories of Albuera and Badajoz, every reader felt that the theme and the treatment were consistent with each other.

As the Light Division accounts for one period of his life, and his *History* for a second, so his advocacy of Sir Charles Napier's excellence in every capacity may be taken for the business of a third. Sir William's devotion to the reputation of his brother, is almost without a parallel. On this point he would brook no question at any hands. In the Ionian Islands, in India, in the command of a home district—wherever Sir Charles Napier was stationed, and whatever he did; his acts were right. The historian of the war in the Peninsula even resumed his pen, for his brother's sake, to write the *Conquest of Scinde, and so wholly must his heart have been in the task, that his alleged preference of this work to his great achievement is not quite incredible.* Even when the life and services of Sir Charles had terminated together, Sir William still stood champion over his grave, and at the most critical period of Indian debates, his chief anxiety was for the reputation of his brother, which, in these discussions, he thought might possibly be impugned. Sir William never proposed to himself an unworthy aim. The image which will remain impressed upon the memory of the public is that of a noble soldier who did his duty in one of England's greatest wars, and who afterwards redoubled this service by raising for his country an imperishable monument of the glory she had acquired.—*The Times, February 13th,* 1860.

---

**X.**

*A New and Cheaper Edition in One Vol., price 12s.*

# The History of the Conquest of Scinde
By Lieut.-Gen. SIR CHARLES JAMES NAPIER, G.C.B.
Written by his Brother, Gen. SIR W. F. P. NAPIER, K.C.B.

---

**XI.**

*New and Cheaper Edition, with Illustrations, price 12s.*
A HISTORY OF

# The Administration of Scinde ;
AND THE CAMPAIGN IN THE CUTCHEE HILLS.
By Lieut.-Gen. SIR CHARLES JAMES NAPIER, G.C.B.
Edited by his Brother, Gen. SIR W. F. P. NAPIER, K.C.B.

---

**XII.**

*Fourth Edition, price 7s. 6d.*

# Defects, Civil and Military,
OF THE INDIAN GOVERNMENT.
By Lieut.-Gen. SIR CHARLES JAMES NAPIER, G.C.B.
Edited by his Brother, Gen. SIR W. F. P. NAPIER, K.C.B.

DEDICATION.
" The Author of this Work is dead.
The care of putting it through the press is mine.
And to
The People of England
It is dedicated;
Because it exhibits faction
Frustrating a great man's efforts to serve the public:
And shows
How surely the Directors of the East India Company
Are proceeding in
The destruction of the Great Empire
Unwisely committed to their
Misgovernment."
W. F. P. NAPIER, Lieut.-General, 1854.

---

**XIII.**

*Second Edition, price 2s.*

# Wellington and Napier.
A Supplement to the above.
By GENERAL SIR WILLIAM F. P. NAPIER, K.C.B.

XIV.

*Price 1s.*

# Napier and the Indian Directors.

### By GEN. SIR W. F. P. NAPIER, K.C.B.

———

XV.

*In One Vol., price 5s.*

# Six Months at Sebastopol;

Being Selections from the JOURNAL and CORRESPONDENCE of the late MAJOR GEORGE RANKEN, R.E.

### By his Brother, W. BAYNE RANKEN.

Contains a valuable narrative of the unfortunate assault on the Redan, in which the writer had the post of honour and of danger, as the leader of the ladder party.

" Major Ranken was a most promising young officer, whose fate it was to be the last Englishman killed in the Crimea. His zeal cost him his life, for having to destroy the large White Barracks, and finding that some of the mines did not explode, he entered them to light the fuse again, and remained buried in the ruins."—*Examiner.*

" Major Ranken evidently thinks the attack on the Redan failed through apathy and bad management. On this question he speaks with great authority. He led the ladder party, and was charged with the engineering operations upon the works. He was one of the first men to reach the Redan, and one of the last to quit it. His narrative has a distinctness about it that we have not found in any other account. The account is long, *but it is an historical document, and the only one,* we believe, that has been published."—*Spectator.*

" Respecting the fearful attack on the Redan, in which he took the lead, he has recorded many incidents which have not yet been mentioned, and which it is only right to make as widely known as possible. A more vivid description, or a more trustworthy account assuredly will never be written. We hope we have done enough (inserting two columns of extracts in addition to remarks) to recommend the best memorial of a thoroughly Christian Soldier which has appeared since the publication of the admirable biography of the late Captain Headly Vicars."—*Bell's Weekly Messenger.*

" The narrative given by Major Ranken, who nobly led the attack, is more graphically told, and evidently more reliable, than any which has preceded it. He is almost the first officer who led 'a forlorn hope' to live to describe what he went through in the performance of so desperate a service. No pen was so competent to place before us, and none has so completely succeeded in doing so, tho attack and the repulse on that occasion."—*Morning Post.*

" Some of the Major's sketches are uncommonly vivid, and being taken from close points of view have a special value. No man was more identified with the dangers of that terrible campaign. We find he was one of the first to enter, and the last to leave the Redan. In trenches and rifle pits, in the forlorn hope and the midnight battle, this brave young officer, in the fulfilment of his duty, gained the respect of all classes in the army. His own narrative, modest and without effort, is precisely such as a soldier should write."—*Athenæum.*

" Major Ranken's Journal is an acceptable contribution to the history of the Siege. His narrative of what he witnessed during that terrible time, 'the Storming of the Redan,' is the most complete and clear account of the affair that has yet been given."—*Literary Gazette.*

" His description of the assault brings the scene vividly before us. We must take leave of Major Ranken's interesting memoir,—it is a valuable addition to our Crimean literature, and the ability stamped upon its pages adds another regret for his loss."—*Press.*

*₊* A few copies only of the two following works, by Lieut.-General Sir C. Napier and Captain King, are to be had of Mr. Westerton.

### XVI.

*Third Edition, price 1s.*

# Volunteer Corps and Militia.

A Letter on the DEFENCE OF ENGLAND. Addressed to each Member of Parliament.

**By Lieut.-Gen. SIR CHARLES JAMES NAPIER, G.C.B.**

---

### XVII.

*Second Edition, price 10s. Plates.*

# Campaigning in Kaffir Land ;

OR, SCENES AND ADVENTURES IN THE KAFFIR WAR OF 1851—52.

**By CAPTAIN W. R. KING.**

" This book is as attractive in style as it is interesting in subject, and in our opinion it has claims upon public attention which cannot be resisted."—*Morning Post.*

" Captain King's book contains the best picture that has appeared of the incidents and hardships which occurred to the troops engaged in the war in South Africa."—*Spectator.*

" To the statesman as well as to the general reader, Captain King affords the most valuable information. His graphic style is admirable. We know of no writer who has crowded so much of interest and importance within the same limits. We have incidents of campaigning ; rapid and forcible sketches of military operations ; graphic descriptions of Kaffir tactics ; delineations of their persons, homes, customs, country, and moral graduation, all presented in a style so unaffected and full of honest energy as to well deserve for Captain King the literary honour of ranking as one of the first authors of his day."—*London Book Circular.*

---

### XVIII.

*In One Vol., price Five Shillings.*

# The End of the Pilgrimage,

AND OTHER POEMS.

**By ELIZABETH MARY PARSONS.**

" Contains some sweet and affecting poetry upon sacred and serious subjects."—*National Standard.*

" Exhibiting feminine tenderness and devotional feeling, lighted up and vivified by flashes of poetical fire."—*Chelmsford Chronicle.*

" Her talents claim for her a favorable notice, and we are induced to hope she will continue to favor the public with her poetical contributions."—*Essex Telegraph.*

" The religious spirit pervading many of the essays is to be commended for its impressive and christian tone. A very acceptable present to the youth of either sex."—*Morning Post.*

" We have here a small volume, but it contains some charming flowers of poetry It is true that they possess the violet hue, and seem to have been written under the shade of the cypress. But what of that ? A pure heart loves to dwell on things in their character sacred, and if *The End of the Pilgrimage, An Old Man's Tale,* and *Twilight,* reflect a subdued and chastened spirit, they are handled with so much delicacy and tenderness, and such pretty imaginary is employed to express the mind of the authoress, that a high tribute of praise must be accorded to this little gem."—*Daily Telegraph, Oct. 20th,* 1859.

" There is a beautiful and tender feeling in these poems, and a sense of religious awe which subdues without extinguishing the natural vigor of the poet's imagination ; the melody of the verse is very sweet, and some of the longer pieces manifestly indicate the power to sustain a higher and wider flight."—*Illustrated News of the World.*

## XIX.

*In One Vol., price Half-a-crown.*

# Christ's Sermon on the Mount,

## AS RECAPITULATED BY SAINT MATTHEW.

A Perfect System of Ethnical Philosophy.

### By NATHANIEL OGLE.

---

## XX.

# Routine ; a Tale of the Goodwin Sands,

## AND OTHER POEMS.

### By ELIZABETH MARY PARSONS.

---

## XXI.

*Fourth Edition, price 1s., with a Postscript and Additional Letter.*

### LADY MORGAN'S

# Letter to Cardinal Wiseman

## ON SAINT PETER'S CHAIR.

" Cardinal Wiseman has had a set-to with Lady Morgan in Italy, and may be said to have been beaten upon his own ground ; Italy being such, by the way, it is a pity he did not stay there."—*Punch.*

" The lovers of our old English style of pamphleteering—that style of which Swift and Junius were the masters, and are now the monuments—will not regret the hour or so required for reading Lady Morgan's Letter."—*Athenæum.*

" The quarrel is worth nothing, if it were only to show what manner of things those are which really do excite the interest and arouse the passions of the new-made cardinal."—Leading Article of *The Times.*

" But to doubt the genuineness of St. Peter's Chair, to discredit that holy relic, shakes that manhood which had stood unmoved by all beside, and causes his eminence to give vent to his feelings in language certainly more forcible than elegant."—*The Times.*

" The terms ' unblushing calumny,' ' foolish and wicked story,' ' truly profligate waste of human character,' ' assassinating of private reputation,' and so forth, are the mild and gentle reproofs which this meek man of Westminster has borrowed from those peculiar purlieus wherein he informs us he delights to dwell, for the castigation and correction of his female antagonist. Nor is his logic much superior to his moderation."—Leading Article of *The Times.*

---

## XXII.

Also, as a Sequel to the above,

*Price One Shilling, with Four Illustrations.*

# The Legend of St. Peter's Chair.

### By ANTHONY RICH, Junr. B.A.

Author of " The Illustrated Companion to the Latin Dictionary and Greek Lexicons," &c.

" Legend, which means that which ought to be read, is from the early misapplication of the terms he imports, now used by us as if it meant—that which ought to be laughed at."—*Tooke's Diversions of Purley.*

## XXIII.

*Price One Shilling.*

# Richelieu in Love;

### Or, THE PROHIBITED COMEDY.

#### By the Author of "WHITEFRIARS." &c.

"'Richelieu in Love'— unusual fact!—is entirely original."—*Times.*

"Written in a sharp, pungent vein, full of sharp rejoinder and searching irony. Anne and Richelieu, whenever they are in contact, maintain a perpetual epigrammati warfare, in which the sarcasms of the Queen are parried by the minister with great dexterity and address."—*Morning Herald.*

"Many of the points are admirable, and as pungent and true as they are witty. Indeed, a smarter or more elegantly written play has not been produced for a lengthened period."—*Morning Chronicle.*

"The language is always appropriate to the characters—sometimes even lofty as the exponent of aphoristic wisdom, or the embodiment of Scintillæ of brilliant wit."—*Observer.*

"The comedy is written in a brilliant epigrammatic style."—*Sunday Times,*

"The dialogue of this play is smartly written, the diction is antithetic, flowery, and satirical."—*Athenæum.*

"'Richelieu in Love' is one of the most brilliant pieces of dramatic writing we ever witnessed, and we notice it here in consequence of the scandalous persecution with which the unknown author has been followed. For nine years this beautiful piece has been refused a license!"—*Racing Times.*

## XXIV.

*Price Eighteenpence.   With Four Illustrations.*

# The Lost Child, and other Tales.

### In Words of Two Syllables.

#### By Mrs. BESSETT,

Author of "The Black Princess," &c.

"No one has a happier knack than Mrs. Besset of writing stories for little people. She weaves fancy and philosophy together in a most attractive tissue; they inculcate a virtuous moral without the irksomeness of pedantry."—*Morning Post.*

"The history is intended as a warning to all other little girls."—*Atlas.*

"It is not difficult to prophesy that these stories will be as great favourites with the young folks as Mrs. Besset's other stories."—*Athenæum.*

## XXV.

*Third and Cheaper Edition, price Three Shillings and Sixpence.*

# Spencer's Cross Manor House.

## By the Author of "TEMPTATION, or a WIFE'S PERILS,"
## "THE NEXT DOOR NEIGHBOURS," &c. &c.

"A charming work for young people—the narrative of the adventures of some children with their attendants at a Manor House in the country; a book for all seasons, but well adapted for a present for young people at Christmas or on New Year's day."

## XXVI.
*Second Edition, price 2s.*

# My Norske Note Book;
### Or, A MONTH IN NORWAY.

The most recent Book on Norway, and full of information of the
most practical kind for the Traveller.

" It is worth while, for those who can afford to do so, to spend a " Month in
Norway," and to take with them, as companion and guide, *My Norske Book.*"
*Literary Gazette.*

" *My Norske Book* is a useful and agreeable addition to the publications upon
these northern regions.—*English Churchman.*

" A pleasant little journal of travel."—*Critic.*

" A pleasant and unpretending little book. It is intended not merely to describe
what the lady saw, but to be a guide to future travellers."—*Illustrated News of the
World.*

## XXVII.
*Price One Shilling.*

# The Aim of the Ministry:
### A SERMON

Preached in the Chapel of the Holy Trinity, Knightsbridge, on
Sunday, January 15th, 1860, on the occasion of Closing the Chapel
with a view to the Erection of a New Church on the same site, by
the Rev. JOHN WILSON, D.D., Incumbent, and Head Master of St.
Peter's Collegiate School, Eaton Square.

---

## XXVIII.
*Price 5s.*

# Descriptive and Explanatory Notes
### ON THE MORNING AND EVENING SERVICES OF THE
### BOOK OF COMMON PRAYER.

### By the Rev. J. E. GOLDING, M.A.,
Late Curate of Hinderclay, Suffolk, but Now Vicar Gurton, Norfolk.

" We must speak of this book in terms of praise; and we think it fills up a
niche not before so well occupied. Mr. Golding's aim has been to aid in
rendering the spiritual use of the Prayer Book more effectual through a more
intelligent use of it."—*Clerical Journal.*

" The conception of the work is good; many of the notes are excellent."
—*Literary Gazette.*

" The title of this work sufficiently indicates the class of persons to whom
it is likely to be useful. The notes are copious and careful."—*Illustrated News
of the World.*

" A careful and well written commentary upon the Liturgy of the Church
such as may be put without fear into the hands of the youngest and less
experienced of her sons."—*Critic.*

---

## XXIX.
*Price Sixpence.*

# Direct and Indirect Christianity.
### A SERMON

Preached on behalf of the London City Mission, by the Rev. LAW-
RENCE MACBETH, in the National Scotch Church, Halkin Street
West, Belgrave Square, on Sunday, February 13th, 1860.

" I have read the Sermon from beginning to end with unmingled satisfaction.
It is a clear and most vital contrast, and I hope it will be extensively circulated."
—*The Rev. Dr. Cumming.*

*27, St. George's Place, Hyde Park Corner.*

## XXX.
# The Strength and Weakness of Christianity.
AN INAUGURAL ADDRESS,
**By the Rev. LAWRENCE MACBETH,**
To the Church of Scotland Young Men's Association, West London
District, Halkin Street, Belgrave Square.

---

# Portrait of the Rev. L. Macbeth.
C. WESTERTON has recently published, at the request of some
Members of the National Scotch Church, Halkin Street West, Bel-
grave Square, as a Token of their regard for their Minister, and
appreciation of his Services, a Lithographic Portrait of the Rev.
LAWRENCE MACBETH. It is admitted by all who have seen it, to be
a most faithful likeness.
It is on View at WESTERTON's Library, where copies, price
*Half-a-guinea,* may be procured.

---

## XXXI.
*Now Ready, in One Vol., price Five Shillings.*
# A Hobble through the Channel Islands ;
Or, the Seeings, Doings, and Musings of one TOM HOBBLER, during
a Four Months' Stay in Jersey and the Neighbouring Islands.
**By EDWARD T. GASTINEAU.**
"It contains enough useful information to render it of service to the public."
—*Critic.*
"This is a lively account of the Channel Islands, and enumerates all that is
necessary to be known."—*Observer.*

---

## XXXII.
*Price One Shilling, by Post Thirteen Stamps,*
# Gen. Sir Charles James Napier, G.C.B.
AS CONQUEROR AND GOVERNOR OF SCINDE,
A Lecture delivered in the Theatre of the Royal United Service
Institution, on Friday, March 30, 1860,
**By COLONEL MACDOUGALL,**
*Commandant Staff College.*
HIS ROYAL HIGHNESS THE DUKE OF CAMBRIDGE, Commander-in-
Chief of the British Army, in the Chair.
"This is a lecture delivered lately in the theatre of the Royal United Service
Institution, by Colonel MacDougall. The lives of the Napiers would furnish
materials for many interesting lectures. In discussing the merits and demerits of
our military chiefs, injustice is frequently done them ; no doubt, this is inseparable
from the freedom of discussion ; the really great, conscious of having discharged
their duties faithfully, will patiently await the fair verdict, which time and the
issue of events will give them. Colonel MacDougall has ably set forth in this
brief lecture the high qualities of the gallant General. Few lives, indeed, afford
such startling and interesting incidents, continuing from the first action in which
he commanded at Corunna, down to the close of his glorious career."—*Lincoln-
shire Guardian.*

## XXXIII.

*Price Half-a-Crown.*

# Mr. Disraeli, Colonel Rathborne, and the Council of India.

### A LETTER ADDRESSED TO

The Rt. Hon. the Lord Viscount Palmerston, K.G.; the Rt. Hon. the Lord John Russell; the Rt. Hon. Sidney Herbert; the Rt. Hon. C. P. Villiers; the Rt. Hon. Sir Charles Wood, Bt., G.C.B.; the Rt. Hon. Sir G. Cornewall Lewis, Bt.; the Rt. Hon. Sir George Grey, Bt, G.C.B.; the Rt. Hon. W. E. Gladstone; the Rt. Hon. T. Milner Gibson; the Rt. Hon. Sir James Graham, Bt., G.C.B.; the Rt. Hon. Sir E. G. E. Bulwer Lytton, Bt.; the Rt. Hon. S. H. Walpole; the Rt. Hon. Sir John Pakington, Bt., G.C.B.; the Rt. Hon. J. W. Henley; the Rt. Hon. Gen. Peel; Lord Henry Lennox; John Bright, Esq.; Richard Cobden, Esq.; John Arthur Roebuck, Esq.; J. B. Smith, Esq.; Thomas Bazley, Esq.; and the other Rt. Hon. and Hon. Members of the House of Commons, in Explanation of a Petition for Enquiry. With a Supplement.

### By COLONEL RATHBORNE.

"That my statements should be received, in the first instance, with incredulity, can cause me no dissatisfaction. Nay, more; I think that, for the honour of human nature, statements of such a kind ought to be so received. Men ought to be slow to believe that such things can happen and happen in a christian country, the seat of almost the oldest European civilization. They ought to be disposed rather to set down my assertions to fanaticism or folly on my part, than to believe them as an over-true tale of the proceedings of a settled government. But though they ought to be thus disposed at the outset, they will not, I trust, bar their minds to the entrance of the light, however painful be the objects it may disclose."—*Letters on the State Prosecutions of the Neapolitan Government, by the* Rt. Hon. W. E. Gladstone, M.P.

## XXXIV.

*Price Sixpence, by Post 7 Stamps.*

# Mr. Disraeli and the "Unknown Envoy."

A Letter to the Right Hon. the Lord Viscount Palmerston, K.G., FIRST MINISTER OF THE CROWN.

### By COLONEL RATHBORNE,

Collector and Magistrate of Hydrabad, in Scinde, from the Conquest of the Province by the late Sir Charles Napier to the 13th of August, 1853.

"Si ces choses qu'ils m'ont reprochées sont véritables, qu'ils les prouvent, ou qu'ils passent pour convaincus d'un mensonge plein d'impudence. Leur procédé sur cela découvrira qui a raison. Je prie tout le monde de l'observer, et de remarquer cependant que ce genre d'hommes, qui ne souffrent pas la moindre des injures qu'ils peuvent repousser, font semblant de souffrir très patiemment celles dont ils ne se peuvent défendre, et couvrent d'une fausse vertu leur véritable impuissance. C'est pourquoy j'ay voulu irriter plus vivement leur pudeur, afin que les plus grossiers reconnaissent que s'ils se taisent, leur patience ne sera pas un effet de leur douceur, mais du trouble de leur conscience."—LE P. VALERIEN, APUD PASCAL.

## XXXV.

*Price Sixpence, by Post 7 Stamps.*

# Exhibition of the Royal Academy of 1861,

### A FAMILIAR AND USEFUL GUIDE TO.

## XXXVI.

*Now Ready, Price Five Shillings,*

# Life of Dr. Orpen,

Founder of the National Institution for the Education of the Deaf and Dumb at Claremont. near Dublin ; and for some years Chaplain to the first Church of the Established Religion of England and Ireland in Colesberg, South Africa.

## By EMMA L. LE FANU,

" Wherever he went he was sure to leave behind him the traces in his path which tell that 'a Christian has passed that way.'"

" This Volume is carefully and well written, and confers honor on the Author as well as the individual whose life it narrates."—*Observer.*

" The career of Dr. Orpen, has been by Mrs. Le Fanu, elaborately chronicled. Far away from those African realms where Dr. Orpen died, a sanctifying voice comes to us from his grave."—*Illustrated News of the World.*

" Dr. Orpen's Life was a source of beneficence."—*Derry Sentinal.*

" Dr. Orpen was an eminent philanthropist—a man, who. like Florence Nightingale, or John Howard, devoted health, strength, and energy, for the relief of an afflicted class of his fellow beings."—*Cork Examiner.*

" Those interested in the amelioration of the condition of the Deaf and Dumb, will read with pleasure this Memoir of the Founder of the first Institution in Ireland for their instruction and relief; the general philanthropist will find other points of character worthy of admiration. The little volume is full of agreeable anecdotes, respecting the different scenes and incidents of Dr. Orpen's varied career, in addition to the portraiture of a singularly amiable man."—*The Globe.*

" These Memoirs are written in a clear, simple, and pleasing style, and indicates clearly enough the benevolent spirit of their subject. No wonder that the kindness of his spirit enlisted the sympathies of all sorts of people in his behalf. Dr. Orpen's own account of his Tiger Hunt, is highly interesting.

" Men like Dr. Orpen, would soon Christianise even the Tribes of South Africa."—*Educational Times.*

" Dr. Orpen takes a high stand amongst the benefactors of the land of his birth, and of humanity; and the unspairing efforts, and unflagging energy by which he effected, from the pupilage of one deaf mute. the foundation of his school, is worthy of the enthusiastic reverence which Madame Le Fanu has brought to her pleasant task."

" Crowded audiences attended Dr. Orpen's Lectures : the exhibition of the attainments of the deaf mute, added to their effect—the audience became infected with the enthusiasm of the Orator."

" But we have not space to enumerate half the good works in which this Philantropist engaged, but must refer our readers to Madame Le Fanu's most interesting volume, which will richly repay its perusal."—*Lady's Companion.*

" Contains a fund of anecdotal matter."—*Record.*

" His career presented a brilliant example of totally unselfish benevolence. His good deeds are at length embalmed in a biography, which should stand on the same shelf with that of Clarkson or of Howard.

" The work ranks high above the common order of such productions.

" In bringing out the principal points of Dr. Orpen's character as illustrative of his chequered life, Mrs. Le Fanu has been entirely successful. In style, the volume is unaffected and touching. Sufficient care has been bestowed upon method in the narrative, and the reader is wisely left to moralise for himself, where occasion arises. Thus, the book is one of the most pleasing description, and we cannot see how any member of the Medical Profession especially, can consider his library complete without such a charming tribute to a noble brother."—*Dublin Evening Mail.*

" Among the Christian philanthropists whom our country has given to the world, Dr. Orpen occupies a distinguished place.

' This noble-minded man '—' this pious and great-hearted Irishman.'

It is, therefore, a source of peculiar gratification to us, that Mrs. Le Fanu has so effectively given to literature the story of this good man's career. The author has manifestly taken great pains with her book. The style is flowing, correct, and vivid. We have not one dull level of circumstantial narration. Light and shade are suitably disposed, and the result is a peculiarly pleasing memoir, which we have not felt surprised to learn that the Irish public highly esteem."—*Dublin University Magazine.*

XXXVII.

*Now Ready, in One Vol. Price 8s. 6d.*

# Cochin-China, and My Experience of it.

## A SEAMAN'S NARRATIVE OF HIS ADVENTURES

During a Captivity among Chinese Pirates, on the Coast of Cochin-
China, and afterwards during a Journey on foot across that
Country, in the Years 1857-8.

### By EDWARD BROWN,

#### AMOY, CHINA.

" The writer of this interesting narrative states that he was a British seaman 'hard up' at Hong Kong in 1856, at the time when hostilities had commenced between the British and Chinese authorities at Canton ; that he obtained a situation in the police force of that place ; and that he subsequently took the command of a native lorcha, with a British registry, bound on a voyage to the west coast, and laden with a cargo of dried fruit and salt. The lorcha was attacked by some pirates off Cape Verela in Cochin-China, and, after an unsuccessful resistance, was captured, along with those of the crew remaining alive after the engagement. The writer was separated from the rest, and, upon the whole, was well treated by the pirates. Soon after his capture, he was appointed gunner to one of the piratical tymungs, and engaged in several attacks upon Chinese junks. On one occasion, he was attacked by the crew under his command, leaped overboard, and swam to shore, where he was at first hospitably treated by the natives, but was afterwards confined in prison at Quong-foo. After a residence of some time among the people, in the course of which he had many opportunities of judging of their modes of life, habits, and customs, he, at length, regained his liberty, and once more set foot on board an English brig. In point of personal treatment, he had little to complain of, for, though restrictions were placed upon his liberty at certain times and places, still, he says, they were only put upon him in order to protect him from injury ; and he very considerately suggests, that if a Cochinese became destitute in England, and received English food, shelter, and clothing, they would be as strange and incompatible to him as their mode of living, habits, and dress were to himself. He expresses himself well satisfied with their conduct, and to the day of his death he will say, ' That the Cochinese generally are a kind and liberal people, and much superior in every respect to their neighbours the Chinese." The narrative is told in an easy and unadorned manner, and affords considerable information respecting a people among whom the French military and naval forces have been, for some time past, seeking to extend the blessings of civilisation, and the knowledge of their freedom."—*Observer.*

" The narrative is one of extreme interest, and bears evident marks of authenticity, with just that amount of style, or the want of it, that gives such a peculiar charm to travellers' tales, whether by sea or land. Mr. Brown's adventures reminds us that we need not go back to the days of the Vikings or the Buccaneers for startling events, dark and desperate deeds, and fearful and horrible scenes, and tales of blood and rapine ; but that they may be found in lands washed by the same ocean that laves the shores of our own territories."—*The Bookseller.*

" This is one of the most interesting and amusing books we have met with for some time. The adventures are narrated in a very spirited manner ; a great deal of acuteness and sagacity in its observation of men and manners is displayed throughout ; and the abundant stores of anecdote and incident make the reader familiar with scenes and country scarcely known to one in ten thousand, and whose political and commercial importance is becoming every day more obvious. Whatever came in his way, worthy of record, the author, who is evidently a shrewd observer, has committed to writing, and the result is a work replete with valuable information, set forth in a very lucid and graphic manner, and as such we recommend it to the study of our readers. The volume is extremely well got up, and reflects the greatest credit both on author and publisher."—*Review.*